A shot rang out

Bolan heard the slug whack into the wall behind him, felt chunks of clay strike his shoulders. He took evasive action, going down on one knee and returning fire. The shadowy figure on the far side of the room flew backward, becoming entangled with a chair and fell hard, blood coursing from his chest and throat. He lay for a while choking on blood and sucking air through his shredded windpipe.

Bolan stayed alert, scanning the room until he was satisfied he was alone. He moved from man to man, checking for signs of life. There were none. He picked up the dropped weapons and threw them in a corner after pulling the magazines.

Then he turned and stepped outside, feeling the heat of the sun as he crossed to the old truck— and the figure bound to it.

MACK BOLAN ®
The Executioner

The Executioner

Don Pendleton's ®

SHADOW SEARCH

A GOLD EAGLE BOOK FROM

W❂RLDWIDE®

TORONTO • NEW YORK • LONDON
AMSTERDAM • PARIS • SYDNEY • HAMBURG
STOCKHOLM • ATHENS • TOKYO • MILAN
MADRID • WARSAW • BUDAPEST • AUCKLAND

First edition January 2004
ISBN 0-373-64302-0

Special thanks and acknowledgment to
Michael Linaker for his contribution to this work.

SHADOW SEARCH

Wrongdoing can only be avoided if those who are *not* wronged feel the same indignation at it as those who are.
—Solon, Athenian Statesman c.638 B.C.

The salvation of mankind lies only in making everything the concern of everyone.
—Alexander Solzhenitsyn, Nobel Prize winner

To those who prey on the defenseless and the weak—beware. I have seen that despair and weakness in your victims and I will not stand aside and abandon them, or allow it to continue.
—Mack Bolan

To all of the coalition military personnel
who have been, or are, serving in the Middle East.
Thanks.

1

Tempala Airport, West Africa.

Phil McReady wasn't a nervous type but he felt slightly uneasy in the presence of the man he knew only as Mike Belasko. Since his introduction to the man at the airport just outside Tempala City, McReady had sensed there was far more to Belasko than the quiet-spoken, reserved persona he displayed. Belasko had stepped off the plane, checking the corner of the airfield that had been allocated to the U.S. team led by Ambassador Leland Cartwright. His manner was that of a man who didn't trust any situation until he had checked it out personally. Because of the presidential authorization given to Cartwright's organization, McReady had been able to take Belasko straight to the waiting car and out of the airport.

Belasko moved with the confidence of a man who knew his way around. His manner belied his physical appearance. Over six foot in height, with a solid physical build, he weighed around two hundred pounds, none of it wasted on fat. He made no play about his appearance. He didn't need to. McReady had also noticed the quiet way Belasko spoke. He didn't raise his voice, yet there was something in his manner that drew good responses from those he did talk to.

As far as McReady was concerned, Belasko was another addition to the U.S. government team in Tempala. That was how he had been told to view Belasko, and to ask no questions. Belasko was also to be given all the cooperation he required—again with no questions asked. It was all on a need-to-know basis. McReady had been given his orders and that was it. The moment Belasko had stepped off the plane, his eyes checking out the area as he walked across the apron to meet McReady, he showed his true calling. This was no man to fool with. McReady made a mental note to keep his curiosity in check. Plain and simple, the message was, do not ask questions and do not get on the wrong side of this man. On the other hand, McReady wasn't an idiot. He knew why Belasko was there. It irritated him because his insider knowledge allowed him the privilege of knowing what had happened to start all this off. The frantic calls to Washington and the U.S. President. McReady had been in on all of it, and then Cartwright had started getting tight-lipped about the whole thing.

In the air-conditioned comfort of the car on the way from the airport to the city, McReady concentrated on his driving.

"So what the hell did they tell you about me, Phil?" Belasko asked. "The way you're avoiding talking, somebody must have laid down the rules pretty hard."

"My boss, Leland Cartwright. He said to meet you at the plane, take you to the hotel and when you're settled in, drive you to meet President Karima. Apart from that I don't question you."

Belasko laughed. "What does he think I'm going to do? Shoot you if I don't like what you ask?"

"I guess we're all a little touchy, Mike. Since Karima's kids were kidnapped things have been a little tense."

"I can see why. Has the lid been kept closed on the situation?"

McReady drew breath, unsure how to handle the question.

"We all know why I'm here," Belasko said. "Karima's children have been taken and the kidnappers are using them as a threat. They don't want Karima signing the agreement with the U.S. because that gives our military a foot in the door in this part of the world. The opposition see that as a means of imposing Karima's authority on the country. They say he'll use the American military to put down any opposition. That won't happen. All we're looking for are deep-water facilities at Rugendi Bay. Refueling and repair units. It will bring in a steady source of income for the country. Karima is also looking for financial backing to regenerate the copper-mining business. Tempala has vast copper deposits and Karima wants to get the business working again. The old regimes have let the business fall apart. I know that and you know that, so talk to me, Phil. I need some intel if I'm going to get those kids back."

McReady smiled. "I'll say one thing for you, Belasko. You can sum up the problem without taking a breath."

"I don't see any reason to walk around the block."

"I guess not."

That summed up Belasko as a whole, McReady decided. The man would tackle anything that came his way in the same manner. Direct, to the point. Given why he was there it was probably the only way to go.

It took just under thirty minutes to reach the city. They drove along a straight, tarmac road cutting through fringes of lush forest and grass. Along the way they passed gas stations and a couple of small settlements. There was a fair amount of traffic.

"Tempala is a nice place," McReady said. "Developing at

a steady pace. Joseph Karima is a good man. Runs a straight government and deals honestly with the people. The only problem he can't get settled is the old tribal affiliations. Africa still has a hell of a time with these blood ties and such. You can have the most democratic government, build houses and power stations, run a stable economy, but it can all be knocked off track by these tribal issues."

"And it's Karima's stumbling block, from what I heard."

"You said it," McReady agreed. "He has an internal struggle going on that's threatening his whole power base. Rebel forces want to turn their backs on everything he's done because they believe it will ruin the country. Damn it, the place was in ruins when Karima came into power. What he's done in twelve years is a miracle. The people have never been so well off and they don't want change. So the rebels have turned to terror tactics. The worst thing they've done is to orchestrate this kidnapping. The way Karima tells it, they want him to step down and hand over all power to the rebels. Allow them to form a new government on their terms."

"How widespread is the news of the kidnapping?"

"As of last night it's still in-house, so to speak. Karima has kept it under wraps. If the news does get out there would be an outcry. Family is everything to this country, and Karima's kids are part of his strength in the eyes of the nation."

"Ten-year-old twins?" Belasko said.

McReady nodded.

"Boy and girl. Randolph and Katherine. Karima's wife died six months after the kids were born. Since then he's brought them up himself."

"What does he know about me?"

"Only that you've been brought in by Ambassador

Cartwright, via the U.S. President. You will handle the affair on your own without interference."

"How does Cartwright know about the kidnapping?"

"Karima trusts him. Cartwright was appointed by the U.S. President to help organize the Rugendi Bay negotiations. When Karima contacted the President and asked for his help the President told Karima he could trust Cartwright. Seems the President and Karima are old friends. Dates back to when Karima was in the States, going through law school. The men and their wives were good friends. As soon as the President heard about the kidnapping he pulled some strings." McReady grinned. "Which is why you're here, I guess."

"Pays to have powerful friends," Belasko observed.

"I'll have to remember that," McReady said wryly.

They reached the hotel. It was a large, modern structure set in cultivated grounds. As McReady drew up outside the main entrance, a uniformed doorman stepped out to open the car door. Belasko carried his leather shoulder bag as McReady led the way inside and up to the reception desk.

The attractive girl behind the desk smiled at him. "Back so soon, Mr. McReady?"

"With a guest," McReady said. "You have a room reserved for him."

"This will be Mr. Belasko?"

Belasko nodded. He signed in and took the key card the girl handed him.

"Fourth floor, Mr. Belasko."

"Thanks," Belasko said as he picked up his bag.

"Meet you here in the lobby in thirty minutes?" McReady asked.

"Fine."

MACK BOLAN TOOK the elevator up to the fourth floor, then followed the wall signs until he located his room. The key card opened the door and he went in, dropped his bag beside the bed and slipped out of his suit jacket. He tossed it on the bed before crossing to the large window. He stared out across the open view of the city. In the far distance he could make out the hazy outline of a mountain chain. He stood at the window for a while, simply enjoying the view.

When he did move he picked up the shoulder bag and placed it on the bed. Taking a small key from his pocket he unlocked the zipper restraint and opened the bag. He reached to the bottom and pulled out a packed shoulder-holster rig. When the rig was unrolled, a handgun was exposed. It was a 9 mm Beretta 93-R machine pistol. He laid the rig on the bed. He took a clean shirt from his leather bag and placed it beside the Beretta. Removing his tie he went to the bathroom, stripped off his shirt and washed up. Emerging from the bathroom, Bolan pulled on the fresh shirt and put on the tie again. Before he slipped into his jacket he put on the shoulder holster.

Checking himself in the mirror on the wall he ran his fingers through his thick black hair, nodding at his reflection. "So let's get this mission on the rails, Mr. Belasko," Mack Bolan said to himself.

24 hours earlier

HAL BROGNOLA SEARCHED the pockets of his jacket for a cigar, sighing audibly when he found one. The director of the Sensitive Operations Group unwrapped it and stuck it between his teeth, looking ready to chew it into oblivion. He looked as if he had resigned himself to the fact that all he could do now was wait for Mack Bolan to make his decision.

The man known as the Executioner, sitting across from the head Fed, was aware of Brognola's agitation. Bolan had been ready to take off on a few days' R&R when Brognola's call had reached him at the ultracovert Stony Man Farm. Within twenty minutes Bolan was on board one of the Farm's helicopters, being flown to Washington by Jack Grimaldi.

"What's up, Sarge?" Grimaldi had asked.

"If I knew I'd tell you," Bolan had answered truthfully. "Only thing I am sure of is I can kiss my vacation goodbye."

"Situation normal then," Grimaldi said, smiling.

"You said it, Jack."

Brognola was waiting for Bolan when the helicopter touched down. The soldier transferred to the big Fed's car and settled back for an explanation. Brognola didn't say a great deal as he drove to a nearby diner. They went inside and ordered coffee.

"Hal, you're looking smart," Bolan observed, taking in the neat shirt and tie. Even Brognola's suit looked as if it had just come off the hanger. "Been to see the head man?"

"As a matter of fact, that's exactly where I've been," Brognola said. "He asked to see me. Urgent meeting."

Their coffee came and they sat drinking until the waitress had moved on.

"Urgent meeting?" Bolan reminded his friend.

"Yeah. The President wanted to ask a favor."

"From you?"

"Christ, Striker, you don't let even me off the hook."

Bolan smiled, shaking his head. "Come on, Hal, we don't need to pussyfoot. What does the man want?"

"You heard of Tempala?"

"On the west coast of Africa. Democratic independent state. The British ran the place about a hundred years ago. President is Joseph Karima. Right now he's in some kind of talks with the U.S. Wants to offer the Navy the use of a deep-water facility. And there's something about copper concessions as well."

Bolan picked up his cup and drank. He waited for Brognola to speak.

"You amaze me. You're right up to date. Karima is going through a hard time at the moment. He's fighting a rebel faction from the Kirandi tribes who are resisting any changes that will benefit the country. These people are doing everything they can to cancel out the deep-water offer and the deal for the copper with U.S. companies. Things are starting to get serious. The rebels have started to use harassment and scare tactics against the general population. Karima has stood up to them until the latest escalation, and that's where we come in."

Bolan saw the look on Brognola's face and knew for sure he wasn't going to like what he heard.

"Just about thirty-six hours ago Joseph Karima's children were kidnapped by the rebels. Karima has been given ten days to agree with the rebel's demands. He must cancel all the negotiations he's involved in and step down from office. If he refuses he doesn't see his children ever again."

"His country or his children," Bolan stated. "Those rebels know how to turn the screw."

"Which is why the President wants us to help," Brognola said. "Striker, Karima is a friend to the U.S. From the mouth of the President, Karima is one of the good guys. He's pulled Tempala out of the dirt and held it together through some really hard times. The future could be good for his whole country if he can complete his negotiations. The copper mining is ready to grow. The deals he has in the pipeline will bring in money and provide jobs. So would the agreement with our Navy."

"You mentioned a favor?"

Brognola rubbed the back of his neck, chewing on his cigar.

"Okay, it's like this. Joseph Karima and the President are good friends. They first met when Karima was in the U.S. at law school. When Karima met the girl he eventually married, the President and his wife were instrumental in helping the relationship along. They were at Karima's wedding in New York. Karima's wife died soon after the children were born. Boy-and-girl twins. Karima brought the kids up on his own and still found time to go into politics and become president of Tempala. It's one of the things the people like about him. Karima is father to his children and his country. Right now the man is hurting. He needs help. Our President has asked for help, Striker. He wants you to go to Tempala, meet Karima and find his kids. All you have to say is yes. A plane is waiting to take you directly to Tempala. Cover has already been arranged. I can fill you in on the way to the airfield. I've got a file in the car. It will update you on everything you'll need to know before you touch down."

Bolan examined his cup.

"The President accepts he'll owe us for this," Brognola said.

"Damn right he will," Bolan answered. "It's going to cost you, too, Hal."

Brognola stared at his friend.

"Big time," Bolan said, smiling. "At least a coffee refill." He pushed his cup across the table.

THERE WAS A CAR WAITING outside the hotel when Bolan joined McReady. They left immediately. The ride through Tempala City was interesting from Bolan's viewpoint. He could see the good Karima had done. Clean, modern buildings stood on each side of the three-lane highway. There were some imposing structures, with a number of them showing American logos. There were a couple of buildings that showed the results of recent attacks. Slogans had been painted across walls, and windows had been broken. A blackened patch showed where a gasoline bomb had been thrown at the building, one belonging to a U.S. mining company.

"Rebels did that a few weeks back," McReady said. "Place had only a week to go before it opened for business. Crazy thing is that all the American companies employ a large percentage of Tempalan citizens. How do you figure it? Someone phoned the local radio station and warned that this was only the start if things didn't change."

"How bad is the rebel problem?" Bolan asked.

"Becoming worse," McReady replied. "They're stepping up intimidation. A lot of it is out of the city and towns, away from the regular law-enforcement areas. Tempala only has a small military presence, and they're spread pretty thin. So the rebels make use of that."

"Sounds familiar," Bolan said. "Only terrorize the people who can't fight back, like the farmers who live in remote areas. How about the mining crews?"

McReady nodded. "Karima is trying to establish the copper production. The deposits here are huge. Which is why he wants an alliance with U.S. mining companies. It would be good for us both. But the rebels are opposed."

Bolan smiled. "They would be."

"Not all Kirandi are with the rebels. There's a big percentage who have crossed the line, put the past behind them so they can improve the country. There are Kirandi in government positions, business. Hell, even Simon Chakra, Tempala's military commander is a Kirandi."

McReady pointed to a building ahead as the car rounded a corner. The straight approach to the government building was impressive. A wide square fronted the building. It was thronged with people enjoying the landscaped lawns and flower beds. Trees swayed in the warm breeze. Government House was a modest affair compared to some seats of power Bolan had seen. It was only two stories high, white and gleaming in the bright day. The car rolled to a stop at the foot of stone steps. Bolan and McReady climbed out. The Executioner followed McReady up the steps to the entrance, where they were confronted by armed soldiers in immaculate uniforms. Before they could respond to the challenge of the soldiers, Bolan and McReady were interrupted by a smartly dressed black man who held out his hands in greeting.

"Mr. McReady, punctual as usual. And this must be Mr. Belasko? Please come inside. The president is waiting for you."

"Raymond Nkoya, Karima's vice-president," McReady said quietly as the man walked ahead of them.

Bolan and McReady followed the man into the building. He led them to a stone staircase and up to the next floor. There they emerged onto a long corridor with offices leading off both sides. All the offices appeared to be occupied. Bolan noticed there were a number of armed soldiers stationed along the corridor.

At the end of the hallway double doors opened to allow them to step inside a spacious office. A desk made from smooth, pale wood occupied a place in front of a wide window that overlooked the square fronting the building. Behind it sat the man Bolan recognized as Joseph Karima. The jacket of his light-colored suit was draped over the back of his leather chair and his sleeves were rolled up. He was in his early forties, handsome man, tall when he stood to step around the desk to greet his guests.

"Phillip, good to see you."

"Mr. President," McReady acknowledged. "This is Mike Belasko."

Karima took Bolan's hand. His grip was firm. "Thank you for coming."

"I hope I can help, sir."

Karima turned to McReady and Nkoya.

"Would you give us some time to talk?"

McReady nodded. "Of course, Mr. President, as long as you need."

Karima closed the doors behind then. He indicated a chair for Bolan and returned to his own. "I am in your hands, Mr. Belasko," he said. "Tell me what you need. If it's in my power you'll have it."

"Photographs of the children would be helpful. Everything you have on the time they went missing."

Karima picked up a file and handed it to Bolan. "It's all in there."

"Did the rebels have help from inside?"

"They were well informed about the children's movements on that day. While it wasn't a state secret it wasn't common knowledge."

"How many of your people had access to that information?" Bolan asked.

From Karima's reaction he realized the man had been taken aback by the question.

"Sir?"

"It never occurred to me that I might have a..."

"A traitor in your camp?"

"So who do I trust, Mr. Belasko? How do I not know that the next person to walk through that door is one of those who conspired to take my children? If I voice my suspicions or point a finger, I risk alerting someone involved. There could be reprisals. Bringing someone into the open could push them into doing something premature. And that would put my children in even greater danger. You understand my predicament, Mr. Belasko?"

Damned if he did, damned if he didn't, Bolan thought.

Bolan sympathized with Karima. The man might have been the commander-in-chief of Tempala, but that didn't render him immune from treachery. Most likely it made him all the more vulnerable. Being in the seat of power placed the man at risk from enemies both inside and outside his sphere of influence.

"I can understand your position, sir."

Karima inclined his head, eyes searching Bolan's face. "Your words suggest you are speaking from experience of betrayal yourself, Mr. Belasko."

"That's another story, sir." Bolan dismissed the subject. "I take it that because you felt exposed and unsure who to trust you decided to ask my President for help?"

"Yes. I traded on our friendship."

"Nothing wrong with that, sir."

"I had to go beyond my own people. A sad indictment of my trust but the way things are I had no other options. We have two tribes, Mr. Belasko, the Tempai and the Kirandi. Centuries of opposition between us. The difficulty is that not all the present-day Kirandi harbor this old tribal culture. They see the world through modern eyes. We have moved on. The Kirandi of today have pushed aside the old ways. Tempai and Kirandi have merged. We all want a new Tempala, free from superstition, looking to the future. If we don't we will all pay the price."

"But not everyone feels that way?"

"Not everyone," he agreed. "Hence our rebel faction."

Karima leaned back, his eyes wandering back and forth across the room. It took him a moment or two to regain his composure.

"Mr. Belasko, how did I fall into this situation?"

"I'd guess you have more than enough on your mind. A lot to handle. It makes you vulnerable. And that is exactly what these terrorists will use to their advantage."

Karima took a deep breath.

"Mr. President, I make no apologies for calling them terrorists. Terrorists attempt to achieve their aims by using the tactics of coercion. Threats. Humiliation of their victims. They terrorize and hope to get what they want by those means."

"My children are everything to me. Always precious but even more so after my wife died. Our children are the future, Mr. Belasko. Why else do we struggle to build a better world? But it angers me that these damned people use them to force me to make Tempala take a step into the past.

"Tempala is not a particularly sophisticated country, Mr. Belasko. We don't yet have the high tech capability of the U.S.A. My security organization is basic. Even our armed forces operate on a simple level. Just men and weapons. Our mechanization runs to trucks, some artillery and a few light tanks. We have no air force to speak of. No satellite communications. In time we may improve but until then we will have to make do with what we can afford. This is why the copper mining is so vital. The contracts will bring in a great deal of revenue, which we need."

Karima stared through the window, watching the people moving about in the square.

"Money will help to improve many things. Hospitals and education. We will be able to upgrade our utilities. More power stations to create electricity. They may seem like simple things to someone from America, but here they are necessities.

"There is a great deal to do, Mr. Belasko. Now it is all under threat from these reb—" Karima turned abruptly. "On second thought, I believe your description is more suitable. Terrorists. They are putting the future of the country at risk."

"These people will use anything to have their demands met. Which is why we can't let them get away with it."

"I feel the same. I refuse to bend to their demands. But then I look at the other side of the coin. How can I risk the lives of my children? Which way do I go? Hold on to my promise to the nation at the risk of losing my children?"

"Not an enviable position to be in, sir, but we're not going to allow it to happen, are we?"

"Are we not, Mr. Belasko?" Karima asked, more in hope than conviction. "God, how I want it to be so."

"Then let's see what we can do to put things right," Bolan said. "Tell me what you need to know."

"First, who knows why I'm here apart from yourself, McReady and his superior?"

"To the rest of my staff you are simply here as an addition to Cartwright's team. You are a security advisor. I have tried to keep the children's disappearance as low key as possible. But I don't know how long I can keep on doing that."

"What about vice-president Nkoya? Your military commander, Colonel Chakra? Do they know the real reason I'm here? And are they aware of the kidnapping?"

"They know nothing more than that you are part of the ambassador's team. In answer to the second part of your question, yes they know about the kidnapping. But they are both under strict orders not to act until I make a decision one way or the other."

"Okay, so let's go back to my earlier question. Who knew enough about your children's movements to be able to furnish the rebels with information?"

Karima considered his answer. He was troubled. Finally he pulled up a pad and picked up a pen. He scribbled across the pad, tore off the sheet and slid it across the desk. Bolan picked it up along with the file Karima had prepared for him.

"If anyone else knew they didn't get the information from me, Mr. Belasko."

"Thank you, sir. I'll start from here."

"If you need me, day or night, use the number I've written down. It's my personal cell phone. I don't give it out very often."

Bolan stood, slipping the sheet of paper into his pocket. As he leaned forward his jacket fell open, exposing the holstered Beretta. Karima saw it, staring for a moment, then glanced at Bolan's face.

"This really is your line of work, isn't it, Mr. Belasko?" he asked.

Bolan closed his jacket. "We're a long way from living in a peaceful world, Mr. President."

"Meet the savage with his own image?"

Bolan smiled. "Something along those lines, sir."

Reaching the door, Bolan turned the handle, then paused to look back over his shoulder. "One thing, sir. How did the terrorists contact you about your children?"

"I received a call on my—" Karima hesitated, the significance only then becoming a reality "—on my cell phone."

2

Back in his hotel room Bolan tossed his jacket on a chair. He crossed to the small refrigerator and took a look inside. There were some bottles of water. He took one and opened it, taking a drink as he settled on the bed to read the file Karima had given him.

The information was scant, direct, and it only took a few minutes to digest. Karima's children had been picked up from his home on the outskirts of the city to be driven to meet Karima. The drive should have taken no more than twenty minutes, but when an hour had gone by, the president received the phone call telling him that the children had been taken. He had ten days in which to carry out the terrorists' demands. If he failed to do so the children would be killed and their bodies returned to him. The terrorists also demanded that news of the kidnap be kept from the media. As proof the kidnappers were serious, Karima was given instructions to check his garage at home. When he did he found his car had been returned, minus the children and with the driver's body in the trunk. The man had been brutally knifed to death, his throat cut in a final gesture.

That had been two days ago. Enough time for the terrorists to travel a good distance from the scene of the kidnapping. Bolan considered the facts, and the more he thought about it the more he became convinced there was an inside connection. He opened the slip of paper Karima had given. There were only three names written on it. Karima had identified one of them as the driver of the car carrying the children. The second was Simon Chakra, whom Karima listed as his military commander. The last name, and Bolan had anticipated this, was Raymond Nkoya.

Vice-president or military commander?

It wasn't beyond the realm of possibility that either of them might be involved. Given the restless nature of African politics, Bolan was aware of the way matters could evolve. There were still undercurrents of tribal loyalties endemic to the African makeup. Civil wars, the struggles between filial groups and the eternal fight against an often harsh land, these were large issues facing the continent. Some countries had weathered the transitions and were growing into stable, forward-looking regimes. Others were still making their way through the troubled times, and in some instances solid regimes crumbled under attacks from within that weakened their power base, sometimes toppling the elected government and allowing an opposition party to gain control.

Joseph Karima looked to be slipping into that kind of maelstrom. It was far from his own making, but he would have little choice if the rebel threat wasn't reversed. They could continue to chip away at his hold on the country, destabilizing everything he was trying to create. Attacks on the infrastructure, the terrorizing of the populace, the slow wearing down of confidence and security, these were the tools of the terrorist. Karima on his own might have weathered all of these things—but now there was an added element. His children. They were being used to coerce him into meeting the rebel demands.

Bolan set aside the file. He found his bag and reached inside for the tri-band cell phone Aaron Kurtzman had furnished him with. Bolan switched it on and waited until it had located the satellite receiver. He tapped the key that speed-dialed the Stony Man number that would connect him directly with Kurtzman's cyber complex.

Kurtzman's gruff tones came through loud and clear.

"Bear, I need you to check out two people for me," Bolan said. "Simon Chakra. He's the military commander here. Then vice-president Raymond Nkoya. Everything you can find out about them. Political leanings. Family backgrounds. As far back as you can go."

"Okay. Anything else?"

Bolan quoted Karima's cell phone number.

"The names I gave you are the only people who should have access to that number. Gives them a direct connection through to Karima. There was a third name. The driver of Karima's car. He was delivered back to Karima's house in the kidnapped car. But he was dead."

"And Karima was told about the kidnapping over this phone?"

"You got it. We may be way off but it's all we have at the moment."

"I'll get back to you."

Bolan picked up the room phone and rang the number McReady had given him. "I may need transport," Bolan told him when the man answered.

"City use, or something to take you farther?"

"Better make it the latter. I might need to go outside the city limits."

"Nice way of putting it. Leave it to me. I'll have something delivered to your hotel soon as I have it ready."

"That's fine."

Bolan replaced the receiver. As he did he felt the room shake. The floor vibrated then the main window blew in, showering the room with glass. He felt something catch his left cheek, a sharp sensation. When he touched his hand to it his fingers came away bloody. All this happened in a micro-second, and following in the next heartbeat came the sound of the explosion. Hot air gusted in through the shattered window. The room shook for long seconds. Bolan could hear rumbling continuing outside.

As Bolan moved to the window, the rumble of the blast fading away, he picked up the rattle of debris banging against the outside wall. More windows had been shattered. People began to shout and scream. Some of shock, others spoke of pain, and Bolan knew there would be casualties. He pulled a leather jacket from his bag and zipped it over his holstered gun as he reached the window. Across the street he saw a dust cloud settling around the remains of a building. The street was littered with debris—and people. Even from his position Bolan could see the mark of bright blood against exposed skin and clothing. He turned from the window and made his way downstairs and out of the hotel.

The building, from his brief moments passing it on the approach to the hotel, had been a shop of some kind. A couple of stories high, with wide display windows showing merchandise. Those windows were gone now, as was most of the frontage. The upper floors were exposed. The street was covered with chunks of concrete, and glass lay everywhere. Cars that had been parked outside the store were half buried under fallen masonry. One was burning, throwing dark smoke into the sky. More smoke was rising from the wrecked store.

No one seemed to be in any state to help. There were a lot of walking wounded. People moving around in a daze, bloody and with clothing in tatters. The concussion had caused many of them to bleed from the ears and nose. They were wandering aimlessly.

Bolan saw his first casualty. A young man struggling to stand, unaware that his right leg was dragging behind him, reduced to bloody tatters. Splintered bone protruded through the lacerated tissue. Blood was pulsing from a severed artery. Bolan knelt beside him, his strong hands settling the man.

"Try to stay still. We'll get help as soon as possible."

Bolan searched for a pressure point, pressed firmly over the spot and managed to reduce a degree of blood loss.

The man stared up at Bolan, his eyes wide with shock. His face was streaked with blood from numerous cuts and gashes. "Why has this happened?"

"Right now we don't know."

The sound of a police vehicle reached Bolan's ears. He looked around and saw a blue-and-white Ford 4x4 rolling to a stop. Armed police officers leapt out, staring around the site of the explosion.

"Over here," Bolan shouted.

One of the officers crouched beside him. He seemed genuinely shocked by the condition of the injured young man.

"We need ambulances. Emergency services. Now," Bolan snapped. "Call it in now."

The officer reached for the transceiver clipped to his belt and began to call in rapid instructions. Two more police vehicles sped into view. Uniformed officers spilled out. One of them was a tall, powerfully built man, with sergeant's stripes on his shirt sleeve. He began to yell orders to the other officers, directing them to specific tasks. The sergeant crossed to where Bolan was kneeling beside the injured man.

"You managing?" he asked, taking in Bolan's bloody hands clamped about the victim's leg.

"For the moment," Bolan answered.

"What a mess," the sergeant said. "Why can't these bastards come out and fight like men? What do they expect to gain from this kind of thing?"

"Confusion. Intimidation. Anything to upset the status quo."

"If I ever get my hands on them I'll upset more than that."

The sergeant glanced around and found himself face-to-face with the young officer who had called in for backup. He was about to yell at the man when he saw the shock etched on the man's face.

"Go to the hotel, Kunda. Tell them we need blankets, sheets and towels," he said in a gentle tone that belied his powerful physical appearance.

The officer looked at him, then turned and headed for the hotel.

"He needed that," Bolan said.

"Ah, youngsters. We were all there once," the sergeant replied.

Over an hour later, Bolan, dusty and bloody, sweat soaking his clothing, leaned against the side of the sergeant's patrol vehicle. He had spent the intervening time helping to pull casualties out of the demolished store. Ambulances were still ferrying the injured to the city hospital. The dead were laid out on the road, covered with sheets. Bolan had counted sixteen. Five of them had been young children. The rescue teams were hard at it, digging through the rubble, searching for others who might still be trapped inside the building.

A group of people was clustered around a car listening to another repeat of the taped message that had been sent to the station within minutes of the bomb blast. The rebels claimed responsibility for the explosion and were threatening more if the government did not accede to their demands. They had been forced into this position because the government had refused to compromise. So the people of Tempala would pay the price. The voice on the tape made the usual excuses, used the same condescending tones as he claimed that what had happened was the fault of a repressive administration. The rebels had been forced to make this dramatic gesture. Not once during the tape did the man even hint at any kind of regret over the deaths of innocent people.

The scenario wasn't unfamiliar to Bolan. He had seen and heard the same in other locations around the world. The work of savages who considered this kind of thing a legitimate part of their agenda. The senseless death and destruction was intended to cow the populace into favoring the demands of the opposition. In Bolan's estimation these people had just crossed the line. They were using the most base form of coercion, and as far as the soldier was concerned, Tempala's rebels—as he had said to President Karima—had stepped into the shadow land that marked them down as nothing more than terrorists.

"They talk as if it's our fault," someone close by said.

Bolan looked up and saw the big sergeant bearing down on him, clutching mugs of steaming coffee in his hands. He handed one to Bolan. The sergeant's uniform was stained and bloody, his black skin streaked with dust and gleaming with sweat.

"That's what they want you to believe," Bolan said. "Make the people feel guilty so they come around to the way of the terrorist."

"Don't you mean our glorious rebels?" the policeman said with more than a hint of irony in his voice.

Bolan looked him in the eye. "No, I mean terrorist."

The sergeant sized up the tall American as if he hadn't quite made up his mind about the man yet. "You know about this kind of thing?"

"A little."

The sergeant shook his head. "I think a lot, my friend."

He stuck out a large hand. Bolan took it and they shook.

"Now tell me who you are. And why you are wearing a gun under that jacket you haven't taken off even in this heat."

There was no threat in the man's tone.

"Name's Mike Belasko. I arrived a few hours ago. I'm part of Leland Cartwright's team. The man who..."

The sergeant nodded. "I know who he his. So, Mr. Belasko, what is your job on the team?"

"Security advisor."

"That would explain the gun."

Bolan smiled. "No fooling you."

"My job."

"You have a name, Sergeant?"

"Christopher Jomo."

"You been a policeman long?"

Jomo gestured at the destruction. "When I see things like this I think too long. Then I remember why I became a police officer and I get angry. Angry at the bastards who do such things. Tempala is not a bad country. Because of President Karima things are getting better all the time. They are not perfect yet, but we'll get there. If we weren't being plagued by these damned...terrorists...we would get there a lot faster."

"Nothing worth having comes without a fight, Jomo."

"I can accept that," the policeman said. "But not when they wage war on children."

Jomo was looking at the five small forms covered by sheets. In death they seemed to shrink even smaller. The big man's shoulders sank and he bent his head for a moment.

"Not the children," he said, almost in a whisper. "Now these men receive no mercy."

No mercy. The policeman's words might have come from Bolan himself.

"You know one of the crazy things here," Jomo said. "Many of the injured are Kirandi. The idiots have killed their own people as well."

"Belasko?"

Bolan glanced round and saw McReady pushing through the crowd. The man looked genuinely concerned when he saw the state of Bolan's clothing.

"Jesus, are you okay?"

"Yes. I've been giving a hand."

McReady recognized Jomo. "I see you two have met."

Jomo smiled. "Mr. Belasko has been a good friend today. It will not be forgotten. I must go and see how my men are doing. We'll meet again, Belasko."

Bolan nodded briefly. He watched the big policeman walk away. Jomo hesitated as he passed the bodies of the five children, and Bolan realized just how badly the man had been affected.

"Hey, you sure you're okay?"

"Phil, don't worry. I just need to get cleaned up."

McReady sensed the hardness in Bolan's words. "Belasko? What is it?"

Bolan took a long, hard look at the death and destruction surrounding them. He listened to the faint cries of the injured.

"This has just become a war," Bolan said and walked away.

BACK IN HIS HOTEL ROOM Bolan used the number Karima had given him and spoke briefly with the president.

"Have you heard personally from the terrorists, sir?"

"I received a call minutes after the explosion. It was a taped message."

"Justifying what they had done?"

"It stated that the bombing was a show of commitment by the rebels," Karima said. "That they meant business. They threatened there could be more of the same."

Bolan considered the implications of the statement. Something didn't sit right. "Why now?"

"I don't understand, Mr. Belasko."

"The ten days they gave you are not up yet. So why suddenly embark on a bombing campaign before they know whether you are going to accede to their demands?"

"As they said, it was to show they are serious."

Bolan shook his head. "I don't buy that. They took your children and murdered your driver. How much more serious does it get than that?"

"Mr. Belasko, what are you suggesting?"

"I'd rather not say anything until I'm sure. I'll contact you again once I have some news."

"Very well. I have to leave now. I'm going to the scene of the explosion, to see for myself what these people have done."

Bolan put down the phone. He was thankful Karima hadn't pressed him on his thoughts as to why the terrorists had set off their bomb. At the back of his mind lurked the possibility that the president's children were no longer a bargaining ploy. Maybe they were already dead and lost as a lever by the terrorists? It was a tenuous strand but one the Executioner had to consider. He knew he was looking at the worst-case scenario—but in his line of work looking on the dark side was a common practice. In this case he hoped it was no more than speculation.

3

Bolan had opened his travelling bag and spread the contents across the bed. His combat gear, blacksuit and boots. His combat harness already loaded and ready for action, the pockets holding additional magazines for the .44 Magnum Desert Eagle as well as the Beretta. A sheathed knife was fastened to the belt of the harness. In one of the pockets was a wire garrote. Another held a number of plastic wrist restraints. He checked the gear, then moved to the Uzi SMG, spending a few minutes stripping it down, checking that everything functioned. The soldier reassembled the weapon, then picked up a double magazine; one magazine taped to another for quick reloading. He snapped the magazine into its slot, cocked the weapon and set the safety. He had two more of the double magazines. These went into the small backpack he had brought, along with a small med-kit and some field rations. There was a canteen he would fill with water from his room fridge before he moved out. Satisfied he had everything he needed, Bolan packed the gear away in the bag and stowed it in the wardrobe, locking it and pocketing the key.

It was now early evening. Since returning to his room Bolan had showered and dressed in fresh clothing. The gash on his cheek had stopped bleeding. It stung occasionally, reminding him of the day's violent event. He decided it was time to eat, so he called room service and asked if they could send him up something light and a pot of coffee. He was promised something very shortly.

Picking up his cell phone Bolan speed-dialed the Farm and waited until he heard the distant connection lock in. The voice that came on was instantly recognizable as Barbara Price's.

"How's it going, Striker?" the mission controller asked.

He told her about the bomb incident.

"Sounds like you walked right into trouble."

"I've had pleasanter days. Has the Bear come up with anything on those names and the cell phone number I gave him?"

"Hold on."

He heard paper rustling.

"Aaron didn't find anything very interesting on either man. They both look clean. Nkoya is down as a loyal member of the government. Backs President Karima all the way down the line. He does a lot of traveling on behalf of the Tempala administration. He was on some kind of government trip about three weeks ago to London and Paris."

"Sounds like a man who moves around a lot."

"I suppose." Price hesitated. "You want to share that with me?"

"Share what?"

"Striker, I know the way your mind works. You can make the most casual remark sound like an accusation."

"Maybe I have a suspicious nature. Go with me on this. Have the Bear dig a little deeper. Look at Nkoya's finances. See if he has anything tucked away. Money. Stock. You know the routine. Same with Simon Chakra, the military guy."

"There's nothing on the cell phone number yet."

"Tell the Bear to stay with it."

"Okay. We'll talk later."

"Yeah."

"Hey, Striker, you take care."

Bolan broke the connection and put the cell phone down. He stood for a while, staring at the phone. Was he being too suspicious? Looking for things that didn't actually exist? If he was wrong no harm had been done. On the other hand...

He heard the tap on his door. Room service. Bolan crossed the room and opened the door. The muzzle of an automatic pistol was thrust in his face.

"Step away from the door," the man holding the gun said.

Bolan eased back, the man following. Without warning Bolan's hands swept up, fingers clamping around the gunman's wrist. The Executioner pulled the man toward him, half turning and throwing the gunman over his hip. The African gave a startled yell as he was hurled across the room. He hit the floor hard, the gun bouncing from his hand. He squirmed over on his back, bleeding from a split lip. He saw Bolan closing in and tried to stand. He barely managed to get his feet under him before Bolan reached him, driving a hard foot into the man's chest that knocked him back down.

The Executioner wondered if the man was on his own and turned to check the open doorway. He caught a glimpse of a dark shape lunging at him, saw the glint of metal an instant before something hard clubbed him across the side of the head. The blow stunned him. Bolan stumbled, fell to his knees, nausea rising. A second blow drove him to the floor, and he felt the room shrink around him, turning black and swallowing him.

BOLAN CAME AROUND SLOWLY, staying still so as not to alert his captors he was awake. He was on the seat of a car by the sounds and movement. He could hear the sound of the motor, feel the bump and sway as the vehicle sped along an uneven road.

There were at least two of them that he knew of. Maybe there were more. It was hard to tell from his current position. He was aware of the pulse of pain in his skull. He could also feel the sticky streaks of blood that had run down the left side of his face from the gash in his temple.

Bolan assessed his situation. He had walked right into the attack. Opening the door without verifying who was there. He made no excuses. The opportunity to check had been in his own hands. His momentary lapse had let his captors subdue him. The next question asked where they were taking him and why? The options were few. They would either question him or kill him. Bolan couldn't see any other variants. Either way his evening looked grim.

He decided that playing dead wasn't going to gain him a great deal. He moved and uttered a low groan, pushing upright on the seat, then flopping against the backrest. Within those few seconds he checked out the passengers. One man behind the wheel, a second sitting across from Bolan on the rear seat, holding a gun on him.

"Wake-up time, brother. Wouldn't want you to waste your last ride missing all the local sights."

"I can live with that."

"That's where you're wrong," the driver said. "You're not going to live at all."

Bolan ignored the threat. He was checking their location. They were speeding along a dusty strip of rutted road between boarded-up buildings. It looked like an abandoned industrial area. Weeds were already choking the empty lots and creeping up the walls of derelict structures. The bush regaining its own. Beyond the rooftops the sky was starting to show red as the sun sank lower. Shadows were spreading.

The car swayed as the driver took a sharp turn, sweeping across a littered area and heading for the gaping doors of a large, empty building. The car rolled inside the cavernous building, coming to a jerky stop.

The gunman nudged Bolan with his boot. "End of the line, brother. Get your white ass out of the car. I don't want to shoot you in here. Makes too much mess."

The driver switched off the motor and pushed open his door.

Backing out of the car the gunman held his autopistol on Bolan, gesturing with his free hand. "You make it faster or I'll change my mind."

Bolan slid across the seat, his reflexes setting themselves for a fast reaction. He needed to move now, not in five minutes, because by then he would be incapable of doing anything.

"Speed it up, Benjo," the driver said.

The gunman—Benjo—glared at the driver for using his name.

The Executioner burst into action the moment the man's eyes flickered away from him. He launched himself off the rear seat of the car, powering himself upright. He grabbed Benjo's gun arm, curling powerful fingers around the man's wrist. Bolan ducked under the gunman's arm, coming up behind the man and snaking his left arm around the man's neck, jerking back hard. Benjo gasped, trying to suck in air through his restricted windpipe. Bolan slid his hand down to the gun in the hardman's right hand, slipping his finger inside the guard, over Benjo's own trigger finger. He jerked Benjo's arm around, lining the muzzle on the driver as the man rushed around the front of the car, reaching for the handgun he kept tucked in the waistband of his trousers.

Bolan pulled the trigger. The autopistol fired, the bullet hitting the driver high in the chest. He stumbled, yelling in pain, his body bouncing off the front of the car. He was still fumbling for his weapon, feeling the pain from the wound, when Bolan fired a second time. This time he took the bullet in the side of his head. The impact knocked him to the ground and he lay in a jerking heap, blood spreading from under his shattered skull.

Benjo, shocked by the sudden, unexpected reversal of roles, struggled in Bolan's grip. He was weakening fast, desperately attempting to suck in air. He offered little resistance when Bolan spun him and slammed him against the side of the car, snatching the pistol from his hand. Benjo felt the muzzle grind into his forehead.

"This can be easy or hard, depending on how you deal with the next couple of minutes," Bolan said.

"I don't know what you want."

"We can start with why?"

"You were interfering in something that was none of your damn business. We took a contract to kill you."

"That answers my second question then. All I need is the name of the one who gave the order."

Despite his position Benjo managed a nervous laugh. "You expect me to tell? You might as well shoot me. I give you names I'm a dead man."

"Don't fool yourself I won't do it," Bolan said. "Your people went over the line when you set off that bomb yesterday.

You killed innocent children in the name of your struggle and expect mercy?"

"Hey, man, I'm no rebel. I just took a job from them. The ones who died in that blast were just unlucky they were in the way."

"Pity they weren't asked if they wanted it that way."

Benjo pushed against the muzzle pressed to his head. His face showed the anger inside. "So go home, Yank. This is not your fight. Go home before you die, too."

Bolan's smile was all the more chilling because it failed to reach his eyes. They were hard and cold, without a shred of pity.

"Tell me what I have to be frightened of? A bunch of back-street thugs who bomb women and children? Real hardmen who can only kidnap the president's young kids because they don't have the guts to challenge him in the open?"

Bolan spun Benjo aside and pushed him away. He leveled the pistol.

"Game's over, Benjo. You had your chance and wasted it. Time's up."

Benjo looked back over his shoulder. Maybe gauging how far he had to go to reach the freedom of the dark night. He even made a tentative movement with his foot. His manner changed abruptly. Benjo dropped to a crouch, yanking up the leg of his trousers, and snatched a slim-bladed knife from an ankle sheath. His arm went back in the first stage of a throw.

Bolan reacted quickly, twisting to one side, bringing the pistol back on line.

From somewhere behind Benjo a handgun fired, briefly illuminating the shadows with its muzzle-flash. The bullet hit Benjo between the shoulders, exiting through his upper chest. The velocity of the powerful slug created a substantial wound, shards of bone mingled with the lacerated flesh. Benjo fell facedown on the concrete floor, his limbs in spasm for a time.

Bolan watched the spot where the shot had come from. He wasn't exactly surprised when he saw the tall figure of Sergeant Christopher Jomo appear. The man was in civilian clothing this time. He came to stand over Benjo, tucking his .44 Magnum revolver into his belt.

"You have a strange way of relaxing, Mr. Belasko."

"I wasn't given any choice in the matter."

"I saw them bringing you out of the hotel."

"Which you just happened to be passing?"

Jomo smiled. "I was on my way to see you."

"About?"

"I was curious. Something made me want to know more about you."

"Such as?"

"The real reason you are here in Tempala. I was just parking my car when I saw those two coming from the rear of the hotel dragging you along with them."

"Lucky for me you have a curious streak."

Jomo glanced at the bodies, then back at Bolan. "I think you've satisfied my curiosity here tonight. Especially why you are in Tempala." Jomo stepped forward. "It wasn't hard to overhear what you were saying. Now I'll tell you something. If the president's children have been taken, let me help. You're going to need someone who knows the country. I was born on a farm and spent my childhood in the bush country."

Bolan held back only for a moment. "What about these terrorists? Any thoughts on where they might take the children?"

"Out of the city, that's for certain. Too many chances of

being spotted if they stayed here. The children are known by the people. They would be recognized."

"Sounds logical. Do they have a base? A central place they operate from?"

Jomo smiled. "My friend, this is Africa, not New York. The whole country is their base. Which is why they are hard to locate. These people live in the bush, move around as they have done for centuries. They can live off the land so they have no need for bases to store their food. They get water from the springs they know or from the water holes the animals use."

"I get the message. So where do we start?"

"In the bush," Jomo said.

"What about these two? Any thoughts?"

"I know the one you shot. Petty criminal. Native Kirandi. Been in prison a couple of times. Has a history of violence. He would have ended up shot sooner or later."

"Any political leanings?"

Jomo shook his head. "He wasn't the committed type. If you are asking if he was with the rebels I'd say no. Most likely he was hired to kill you because he was on the spot."

"Pretty much what I heard."

Jomo bent over the man and searched his pockets. He stood up again, waving a thick roll of banknotes. "Check Benjo. He'll be carrying the same. He was a brother criminal."

Bolan found a similar roll of bills. He threw it to Jomo.

"Plain and simple, Belasko. They were paid to make you disappear."

As THEY DROVE BACK to the hotel in Jomo's battered Land Rover, Bolan told the sergeant about Karima's kids. He knew he could trust Jomo, and he needed someone with Jomo's knowledge on his side. The light was starting to fail by the time they reached the hotel. The hard heat of the day had begun to fade as Jomo parked in a dark corner of the parking lot. Bolan went in and up to his room. Nothing had been touched. His captors had even closed the door when they had left, taking him with them. They must have used the fire escape to avoid being seen. He took the shoulder bag from the wardrobe. Bolan stripped and pulled on his blacksuit and boots. He spent a few minutes in the bathroom doctoring his head wound. He packed his weapons and gear into the backpack, then filled the canteen with water from the fridge. Slipping his cell phone into one of his zippered pockets he left the room and made his way back downstairs, using the fire escape. He walked around the side of the building and rejoined Jomo.

The policeman took a look at the blacksuit. "Now you dress for business?"

"Something like that," Bolan replied.

4

Jomo drove first to the area where Karima's house was situated. He kept up a steady speed so as not to alert the security men stationed around the property.

"We should go that way," he stated, pointing along the street. "Out of the city. If I had Karima's kids that's the way I'd go. Up country, into the bush. And I'd keep going until I was in rebel country."

He kept driving, passing other houses, each with its own large grounds.

"They would go this way," Jomo said. "To the places they know and where they can hide. And they will have friends out there. Their followers."

Bolan studied the far-reaching spread of the empty plain. It was mostly flat land in the region, though there were mountains to the north and some hills in between. Between the plains and the mountain range, according to Jomo, there were great swathes of deep forest country.

"Give it your best shot, Jomo."

The African nodded and set the Land Rover along the road. They traveled for a couple of miles until the last of the houses were well behind them. Then he slowed the SUV, stopping a couple of times to climb out and check the edge of the road. The third time he did it he beckoned for Bolan to join him. There was a full moon. It cast a pale light across the land, allowing them to see reasonably well.

"A four-wheel drive vehicle left the road here," he said, indicating faint marks in the dust. He squatted on his heels, staring down at the tracks. "Since the kidnapping the weather's been pretty calm. Not a lot of wind so these tracks haven't been filled yet. I say they are two days old. No more."

Bolan studied the tire marks. There was no doubt they had been made only a couple of days ago. Jomo's evaluation rang true. If the tread marks had been any older they would have been obliterated by now. The edges were dry and starting to crumble, some of the upper rims starting to fall in.

"One good gust of wind and these are gone," Jomo said.

"Heading straight north," Bolan said. "How far to the cover of the forest?"

"Three days' steady travel before they reach the hard growth. They would have to leave the vehicle then. Go on foot. The forest is too dense to drive through. That's if they go that far. They might have a rendezvous point closer. Somewhere out in the bush."

Jomo pushed to his feet and followed Bolan back to the Land Rover. They climbed in and Jomo started the motor, swinging the vehicle around and driving off the road. The tires sank into the dusty ground. Jomo pushed down on the gas pedal and the SUV surged forward. They drove for a while before Jomo spoke.

"I don't think they'll use the forest. More likely to stay on the plain and use the villages to the north. The tribes who back the rebels occupy that region."

"You know them?"

Jomo laughed. "Know them? I'm from the Tempai tribe. Karima's people. The rebels are Kirandi. The two tribes have been at each other's throats for decades. Things don't change as fast once you leave the big cities."

As full darkness fell and the moon vanished behind clouds, Jomo switched on the headlights. The powerful beams cut through the gloom. Even in the dark Jomo seemed to know where he was going. The ride was bumpy. Land Rovers were not designed for smooth riding and every jolt and bounce was transmitted to Bolan's spine. They drove at a steady speed for the next three hours. Bolan was silently grateful when Jomo rolled to a stop and cut the motor.

The night was alive with the chatter of insects and the deeper sounds of animals. There was little chance of concealing the vehicle out on the flat, featureless plain so they didn't bother.

"It's safer to sleep inside the vehicle," Jomo said. "You want the front or the rear?"

"I don't care," Bolan answered.

From the equipment in the rear of the SUV Jomo produced blankets. He tossed one to Bolan. He also produced an SA-80 carbine, a short version of the British SA-80 battle rifle, chambered for the 5.56 mm round. This second version of the carbine was capable of taking 30-round magazines from the M-16. It was a sturdy, hard-wearing weapon, and though it had failed to excite the British military as had its predecessor, the SA-80 carbine had found its own market by being sold abroad. There were a bunch of long, beautifully marked feathers fixed to the stock, held in place by tight rawhide thongs. Jomo noticed Bolan studying the feathers.

"From an eagle. Took them myself when I was younger. I kept them all these years, part of Tempai tradition." The African laughed. "You see, Belasko, we are all still held by our beliefs."

"Eagle feathers beat murdering children any day," Bolan said.

The soldier took time to remove his 9 mm Uzi from his bag before he pulled his blanket round him and settled in the passenger seat.

"I'll take first watch," Bolan said. "Wake you in a few hours."

Jomo sighed. "I knew you were going to say that," he grumbled before he settled himself down to catch some sleep.

Bolan cradled the Uzi across his thighs. He gave himself time to adjust to the African night, his eyes gradually focussing on distant shapes and the deeper shadows that enveloped them. He could distinguish between solid objects and the false shapes formed from light and dark. It was easy to become fooled by imaginary shapes, believing them to exist until close examination identified them as nothing more than illusions. He changed his line of vision often, not allowing himself to concentrate on one spot for too long. When the eyes became fixed on one spot it was not unknown for the mind to start seeing things moving. Inanimate objects took on a phantom life, seeming to shift from spot to spot. The mind, the night, and the boredom that could set in during long sentry spells combined to distract the man on duty. It was all too easy to fall under the spell.

Bolan thought about Karima's children. What would be going through those young minds? Snatched from their normal existence to be dragged off into the wilds, surrounded by strangers who, on their own admission, were opposed to everything their father stood for. It would be a far from pleasant episode. The other side of the coin might ease the burden for them. Children were resilient beings, often showing a surprising tenacity when placed in dangerous situations. Bolan hoped that Karima's son and daughter would be able to exhibit those characteristics.

Thinking about the children brought his attention back to the bomb incident. He hadn't voiced his real feelings about it to Karima. That the terrorists had set off the bomb because they might no longer have the children as bargaining chips. The unexpected turn of events, coming in the middle of the kidnap process didn't gel as far as Bolan was concerned. Why make such a dramatic gesture when they already had their lever? He accepted that trying to fathom the terrorists was difficult. They were by definition unstable and liable to unexpected changes in their procedures. But he still felt the bombing had come out of left field.

The soldier didn't dwell on the matter for too long. Speculation only led to confusion. If there was a logical reason behind the bombing it would reveal itself in time. It wouldn't be hurried no matter how long Bolan deliberated over it.

As the night closed in, the heat of the day slipped away, replaced by a noticeable chill. Cold air coming in from the west, drifting in from the coast. Bolan pulled his blanket tight over his shoulders. Behind him he could hear Jomo's heavy breathing. The African was taking full advantage of his time out.

An hour passed. Bolan had just checked his watch when he heard the gentle, insistent sound of his cell phone. He took it from his pocket and accepted the call.

"Did I wake you?" Aaron Kurtzman asked, without a trace of regret.

"No," Bolan said. "I felt guilty keeping you awake so I decided to sit up all night."

"It's called teamwork," the computer expert replied. "Okay, we ran more checks on your people out there. Can't find a damn thing out of place as far as the vice-president is concerned. If he's off the rails he's keeping it well hidden."

"Okay."

"Simon Chakra on the other hand," Kurtzman went on, then paused. "You still awake?"

"What do you think?"

Kurtzman chuckled.

"Native Kirandi. He's been in the army since he was big enough to hold a rifle without falling over. He came up through the ranks, then went to the U.K. to complete his officer training, as a lot of African officers seem to do. I got into some reports written about him by the officer school. It seems our boy always had a thing about Tempala's national identity. Back then he talked a streak but didn't show any radical tendencies. It was written down as a sort of home-boy zeal. He went back to Tempala and worked his ass off in the army. Good combat record during some internal strife over ten years back. Good officer. So much so that when Karima was made top man he promoted Chakra to military commander. Chakra has never been shy at declaring his full support for Karima and his policies."

"All sounds good, Bear."

"I'll bet Karima doesn't know about his boy having an account in the Cayman Islands. Cash deposits over the last few months. The guy has close on three and a half million in U.S.

dollars. It also seems he was seen in the company of two Cuban advisor-types on an unofficial trip to Havana last month. One of our covert units in Cuba spotted him in deep talks with these guys at a villa just outside the city. They keep watch on anything happening in Cuba, take pictures and send them through to their agency. No one had recognized Chakra until a few days ago. On the global scale he's not a real player. Sit him back down in Tempala, I guess you'd have him a good way up the ladder."

"Be interesting to find out if any of the so-called rebels from Tempala have been cosying up to Castro's advisors," Bolan said.

"Way ahead there, Striker. I did some more trawling and came up with IDs on two Tempalan nationals. Rudolph Zimbala and Shempi Harruri. They are part of the ruling council of the rebel faction. Both have been mixing with our Cuban buddies. The same faces cropped up from the pictures taken with Chakra."

"Any feedback on what they were discussing?"

"The covert team was unable to get any sound bites, only the images. But the data they sent back to home base was that one of the Cubans was seen with all three of their visitors, one Hector Campos. He is an advisor in the organization and promotion of internal resistance. Just what Tempala is going through at the moment."

"Thanks, Bear," Bolan said. "You come up with anything else let me know."

"Can't pick up anything on that cell phone number, but I haven't given up yet. Soon as we can grab a bird I'm going to run some satellite surveillance over Tempala. See if we can pick up anything that might suggest what's going on."

BOLAN SAW OUT HIS WATCH, going over the information Kurtzman had furnished him with. Did the disclosed facts about Simon Chakra point to him being the man behind the kidnapping of Karima's children? The man would certainly have been privy to the comings and goings of the president and his family. Those facts on their own didn't make the man guilty. But they put him in the frame. Chakra would need watching until the facts could be confirmed.

It was coming up to one a.m. when Bolan roused Jomo. The policeman climbed out of the Land Rover and walked around to stretch his legs. He rummaged in the rear of the vehicle and produced a pack of plastic bottles holding mineral water. He took one for himself and handed a second to Bolan.

"You should have woken me before this," Jomo said, glancing at his watch.

"No sweat," Bolan replied.

The soldier took his place in the rear of the Land Rover, finding a reasonably comfortable spot. Bolan took a drink from the bottle, only then realizing how thirsty he was. He pulled the blanket around him, keeping the Uzi close and settled down to get some rest. A little while later he felt the Land Rover rock gently as Jomo climbed in and took his place in the passenger seat. Bolan let himself relax, sleep coming quickly.

It seemed only minutes later when he felt Jomo's big hand on his shoulder. The African was shaking him.

"Belasko. Wake up, Belasko, we have visitors."

Bolan woke quickly, the Uzi ready for use as he sat upright, the blanket slipping from his shoulders. It was already well into the dawn. Pale light flooded the plain. Somewhere close by birds erupted from thick brush, wheeling and swooping as they rose into the air. The sound of their passing came as a soft rush of feathered panic.

"Stand beside me," Jomo said.

He was at the front of the Land Rover. He carried his SA-80 carbine with the butt resting against his hip. He stood motionless except for his large head, which moved back and forth as he scanned the close terrain. Bolan moved up alongside, Uzi in plain sight but not at a threatening angle.

"They will come out when they are ready."

Off to the right the high brush shivered slightly. A hint of movement but enough to indicate that someone, or something was in there. Bolan spotted the disturbance but made no indication. He stayed as still as Jomo, aware they were being observed by an unseen viewer.

"Any idea who they are?" Bolan asked.

"Some of my people. One of the Tempai tribes. My people were farmers. These are bush people. Nomads. They move from region to region with their cattle. When the grass is used up in one place they seek another. On and on through each year. By the time they return to where they started the grass has grown again. It is the way they have lived for hundreds of years. Other tribes across Africa do the same."

"Are they friendly?"

"Yes, but cautious. If you had come here with your own cattle you would probably be dead by now."

"Territorial people?"

"Very much so." Jomo paused. "They're coming out."

Bolan saw the Tempai appear from the bush from a number of locations around the Land Rover. They were tall, lean, with skin as black as ebony. They were clad in bright, patterned robes that seemed to be casually draped around their bodies. Simple pieces of jewelry adorned their wrists and ankles. Each man carried a long, slender spear which he held across his chest, resting against his left shoulder. Bolan noted that there were feathers similar to Jomo's tied to the shafts of the spears.

"The position of the spear lets you know how they feel about you," Jomo said. "The way they have them makes it difficult to use quickly so they are telling us they mean us no harm."

"How would we know if they did mean us harm?"

"Man, they would throw the bloody things at us," Jomo replied in a matter-of-fact tone.

The Tempai formed a loose half-circle in front of Bolan and Jomo. One them made a casual move with his free hand and launched into a fluid, lilting address. Jomo listened in respectful silence until the man had finished. Before he replied, the policeman showed his weapon to the Tempai, then slung it from his shoulder, muzzle down. He spoke directly to the tribesman who had delivered the speech, in their own tongue. When he had finished the Tempai spokesman nodded enthusiastically, turning in Bolan's direction. He held out a long arm, hand held palm out.

Bolan slung his Uzi as Jomo had done, then stepped forward and greeted the Tempai with his own raised hand. There was a chorus of approval from the watching tribesmen.

Jomo spoke again, indicating Bolan a number of times in his speech. When he received his reply he glanced across at Bolan.

"They have invited us to join them for breakfast."

Bolan nodded in the direction of the Tempai. They moved forward, clustering around the black-clad American.

"They have never seen a white man dressed like you before. They believe you are a warrior. A fighting man from across the ocean. But they still want us to join them for break-fast. They are curious about you."

"Jomo, they wander all over this region. Maybe they saw something."

"Like rebels with two children in European clothing?"

"Exactly."

"I'll ask. But first we have to do the breakfast thing. If we refuse they will be offended."

Bolan and Jomo followed the Tempai in the Land Rover. The tribesmen wandered through the spreading bush, seemingly on an erratic course. After almost a half hour they emerged in a wide, dry basin that was at least a quarter mile in diameter. There was a small water hole in one section, with some grass growing in the vicinity and a herd of pale-skinned cattle with short horns grazing on it. The cattle looked underfed, almost scrawny to Bolan. He was used to seeing American beef herds that were comprised of hefty, well-nourished animals. He had to remind himself that he was in a totally different environment.

They had emerged close to the Tempai campsite. Being nomadic the Tempai had little in the way of permanent homes. They carried whatever they owned from region to region. Tents made from hide and stretched over wooden poles pro-vided shelter for the men and their families. There were women and children in the camp as well as suspicious dogs that ran about in excited packs, yapping at everything in sight. Smoke from a number of communal firepits rose in the cool morning air. There was little wind at this hour and the smoke hung in pale spirals, tingeing the air with acrid smells.

Jomo braked and switched off the Land Rover's motor. He stepped out, still carrying his carbine.

"You hungry?" he asked as Bolan walked at his side.

"The menu will probably decide that," the soldier answered.

They were invited to sit at one of the firepits. A group clustered around, led by the man who had done all the talking at their first meeting. Women and children joined them.

"You realize that these people are a good chance for us to gain information," Jomo said.

Bolan glanced at him and the African was smiling. "So?"

"So we can't afford to upset them."

"Okay. So what does that mean?"

One of the Tempai handed a shallow clay bowl to Bolan. It held a number of fat white grubs. They were still alive, moving sluggishly.

"My fault for asking," Bolan said. He took one of the grubs and held it up so the Tempai could see it.

"Full of goodness," Jomo stated, a huge grin on his face.

Bolan ate the grub, refusing to ask what the goodness consisted of. He was sure the thing was still wriggling when he swallowed it. The rest of the meal was less dramatic. Fruit picked from the bush. Meat resembling chicken that Bolan was convinced spent its life crawling across the earth hissing at people.

The assembled Tempai chattered and joked. Some of the translation was lost on Bolan because Jomo appeared to be enjoying himself. It was later that Jomo directed a specific question to the Tempai spokesman. The man considered for a moment before he nodded and replied, gesturing in a particular direction.

"Ashansii says two days ago they saw a truck driving by. There were men inside with guns. And two children in city clothes."

"Boy and girl?" Bolan asked.

Jomo's question brought nods from a number in the group. There was more talking, everyone trying to speak at once. The one named Ashansii held up his hands to silence them, directing the questions at Jomo.

By the time it was all over Bolan knew they had the right party. The timing was right and so were the descriptions.

"They were heading north," Jomo translated. "It's the direction I'd be going if I was those rebels."

Ashansii came to Bolan and touched his shoulder, saying something to Jomo.

"He is asking what you are called."

Bolan faced the tall African. "I am Belasko."

Jomo translated.

"Be-las-ko," Ashansii repeated. There was a chorus of approval. Beaming smiles and nods in Bolan's direction.

"Time we moved out," Bolan said. "We need to close the gap."

Jomo nodded. He took a long look at the brightening sky, taking in the cloudless blue. "Belasko, it's going to be a hot one."

Bolan didn't answer. Something had told him that already. And he wasn't thinking about the weather.

5

Two hours after leaving the Tempai tribesmen, Jomo pulled the Land Rover to a halt below a dusty ridge. He cut the motor and reached for his carbine.

"About a quarter mile beyond the ridge is a small village. The rebels have often used it as a supply base. Food and clothes, not weapons. This is a poor place. The people help because they have no choice. So there will be no love lost between them and the rebels."

"Are they Tempai or Kirandi?"

"Kirandi. Even out here not every Kirandi agrees with the rebels. Some have no choice. They help or they suffer. Either way they lose."

Bolan grabbed the Uzi. "Just a precaution."

Jomo started the engine and drove the Land Rover across the ridge and down the far slope. Dust billowed in their wake, despite the policeman's driving at a slow speed. They leveled out and moved toward the village. It was as Jomo had said, a poor settlement. The scattering of huts was constructed from mud and thin poles. There was an air of desperation around the place. Bolan saw a few pole corrals holding cattle. A few bedraggled chickens wandered the spaces between the huts, searching the dusty earth for food. The usual skinny mongrel dogs prowled around, sometimes making half-hearted attempts at chasing the chickens. Smoke from cooking fires rose into the still, heat-hazed air, hanging at roof level.

As Jomo pulled into the center of the village, figures moved into view. They were dressed in simple clothing, all of which looked as if it had been around for a long time. The inhabitants approached the vehicle, watching Bolan and Jomo with undisguised suspicion. None was armed.

Bolan stepped down from the Land Rover, his Uzi hanging at his side. He remained where he was, returning the stares from the villagers.

Jomo spoke to the gathering crowd. He received little response until something he said jolted one man to reply. He carried on a conversation with Jomo for a while. The policeman beckoned the man to come forward.

"They were here," Jomo said to Bolan. "Same description we got from the Tempai. They stayed long enough to pick up water, then cut off for the north."

Jomo brought a tattered map from the Land Rover and spread it across the hood. He indicated a spot. "We're here. If the rebels stay on a northerly course they have to cross the river here and then cut through this valley. Once they do they're in rebel country for certain."

"With the lead they have that must have already happened," Bolan said.

"Probably," Jomo responded.

"The money we took from those two back in the city," Bolan asked, "you still have it?"

Jomo nodded, smiling. He took the bundles and handed them to the villagers, speaking to them as he did.

The money was received and quickly hidden from sight.

"What did you tell them?"

"That President Karima has sent it as a gift to his people. So they can use it to make village improvements."

"Think they believed you?"

"Not a bloody word," Jomo said, grinning widely.

A stir of sound came from the gathered villagers. Bolan turned and saw them pointing skyward. He followed the pointing fingers and saw the dark speck that was growing rapidly. He fixed his gaze on it until he was able to identify the outline of a single-engined plane.

"The rebels have any aircraft?"

Jomo shrugged. "Military does," he said. "Maybe they're working with the rebels."

"What makes you say that?"

"In my line of work you hear things. Unrest in some of the remote units. We've been investigating rumors about weapons going missing from storage depots. That kind of thing. Nothing definite but it makes a man start to think. You know what I mean?"

With the suspicions Bolan had about Tempala's military, following his discussion with Kurtzman, the possible presence of a military spotter was less than welcome news.

"Jomo, let's move out. I don't want anything to happen to these people because of us."

To his credit Jomo didn't waste time. He scrambled back behind the wheel of the Land Rover, his map fluttering behind him as he gunned the motor and set the vehicle into motion. He drove through the village and out across the open land.

Bolan scanned the sky, shielding his eyes against the hot glare of the sun. He picked up on the aircraft as Jomo sped them across the plain, the SUV jolting them at every pothole and rut in the hard, baked earth. He watched as it made a wide, lazy sweep that brought it directly ahead of them. The plane dropped low, skimming the tops of scattered trees as it hurtled toward them.

"This is not good, Belasko," Jomo said.

The plane's pilot showed his hand too quickly. The stuttering crackle of machine-gun fire ripped across the plain. The earth erupted as twin lines of fire gouged the hard ground. Jomo held the Land Rover on its forward course, turning the wheel only at the last moment. The plane flew over them, climbing rapidly, the sound of its powerful engine echoing in its wake.

"He's turning," Bolan said, twisting in his seat to watch the plane.

He had it identified now. An Embraer EMB-312. A Brazilian aircraft designated Tucano. The machine could be equipped with rocket pods as well as machine guns. There was even a bomb-carrying capability.

"Those markings are military," Jomo said. "He comes from a base some way up-country."

"Can we find some cover?" Bolan asked as Jomo hauled the Land Rover back on line, shoving his foot down hard.

"I'm looking, but don't hold out too much hope. There aren't too many caves around here."

Bolan clambered into the rear of the Land Rover, bracing himself against the exposed canopy frame. He brought the Uzi up to his shoulder, watching the Tucano as it lined up for another run. This time it was coming in on the Land Rover's rear.

Bolan didn't expect to do much damage with his Uzi, but he might make the pilot decide on a little caution.

The SUV hit a deep rut. The rear end bounced hard, almost jolting Bolan out of the vehicle. He hung on with one hand, feeling the Land Rover sway, veering left and right as Jomo fought the wheel. There was a heart-stopping moment when the left-side wheels lifted off the ground. Bolan swung himself to the other side of the vehicle, adding his weight to Jomo's. The vehicle returned to earth with a thump.

The attacking aircraft came at them in a blinding rush, looming large.

Bolan braced his Uzi on the vehicle's tubular frame, judging angle and velocity. His finger stroked the trigger and the Uzi crackled. The moment after he'd fired he adjusted his aim and triggered again. He saw a brief flash of sparks as some of his 9 mm bullets clipped the edge of one wing. The hit was minor, not enough to incapacitate the aircraft, but it made the pilot yank back on the stick and take the plane away from the Land Rover. Even so the pilot released a small bomb. Bolan saw the dark shape as it tumbled end over end, hitting the ground and bouncing, its trajectory bringing it closer to the SUV with every second.

"Jomo, hard left!" Bolan yelled. "Now!"

The Land Rover lurched violently. Bolan was hurled to the right. He slammed up against the spare cans of diesel fuel that Jomo carried strapped to the inside. The impact stunned him for a few seconds.

The bouncing bomb flew past the Land Rover, then exploded in a boiling mass of flame. It was an incendiary device. The ball of flame spread across the plain, leaving a black, oily smear in its wake. Some of the gelatinous material smeared the right side of the Land Rover, igniting, and left the racing vehicle with a fiery tail.

Jomo was yelling something unintelligible to Bolan. The Executioner couldn't be certain whether the African was cursing the pilot or expressing his alarm at the sudden, violent turn of events.

The Land Rover dipped suddenly as a steep-sided dry watercourse appeared before them. Jomo took the vehicle down the slope without any thought for caution. They hit bottom with a hard thump. Jomo spun the wheel and stepped on the gas, swinging the Land Rover along the rocky, rutted base of the watercourse. He brought it to a shuddering halt among a tangle of thorny brush, cutting the motor and leaping out to scoop handfuls of dirt at the flame that was still scorching the paint work. Bolan joined him and they put out the fire.

They stood motionless, listening for the drone of the aircraft engine. After a few moments they picked it up. The sound wavered, fading, then rising again. It became louder.

"He's coming back," Bolan announced.

He moved away from the Land Rover and worked his way up the slope, flattening out near the top. Jomo dropped down beside him, his dark face gleaming with sweat. Neither spoke as they scanned the sky, searching for the Tucano.

"There he is," Bolan said, pointing.

The aircraft was about a quarter mile out, almost gliding as the pilot located his former course and followed it in to where the incendiary bomb had left its mark. The fireball had all but gone now, leaving only a black curl of smoke.

Jomo checked his SA-80 carbine.

"Five years I've had that Land Rover. Never got one scratch on it," he said bitterly, then quickly added, "okay, there were a few marks when I bought it, but military or not, that son of a bitch is in trouble."

The Tucano throttled back as the pilot brought it in lower, skimming the ground so he could get a better view of the place where the bomb had detonated.

"He's checking to see if he actually hit us," Bolan said.

The only response from Jomo was a short grunt. He was belly down, the SA-80 snug against his shoulder as he took aim. He held the target for long seconds before he eased back on the trigger, firing three times in rapid succession. Bolan saw the point of impact where two of the 5.56 mm bullets ripped through the Perspex canopy. The pilot lurched forward, then powered up his engine, the Tucano banking violently to the left, swinging in toward the dry watercourse. It was only forty feet above the ground as it came directly at Bolan and Jomo. The machine guns opened up, raking the earth. Bolan leaned across and shoved Jomo to one side, sending him slithering down the slope, then pulled himself out of the line of fire. There was a roar as the aircraft closed on their position. Dust filled the air, showering Bolan with gritty debris. The engine sound was overwhelming. The Executioner rolled on his back, pushing the Uzi into a vertical firing position, and pulled the trigger, holding it there as the blurred outline of the Tucano went by. The downdraft from the propeller sent clouds of choking dust into the watercourse, blinding Bolan for long seconds. He slid down the slope, coughing, his blacksuit caked in dust.

The Tucano vanished, trailing a thin stream of black smoke, climbing as the pilot regained full control. It became a tiny speck, lost in the hard blue expanse of sky, then the sound of the engine faded, too.

"I think we hit him," Jomo said. He used his sleeve to wipe the dust from his face, spitting out the dry pasty taste from his mouth.

Bolan nodded. "If he's in contact with any ground force he'll be radioing our position right now."

"Belasko, I want to know what the hell is going on. Why is the damned military shooting and bombing us?"

Bolan didn't reply for a moment, giving Jomo time to digest what he had just confirmed.

"Okay, okay, I know what I just said. That bloody plane had the markings of the Tempala military on it. Yes, I saw it, and I don't know why that pilot was trying to barbecue us. But I've got a feeling it's because of you, Belasko."

"I'll tell you what I know, Jomo, but let's get out of this damn watercourse first."

They returned to the Land Rover, Jomo shaking his head when he examined the burned paint work. He started the engine and reversed, then drove up out of the watercourse with the expertise of a man who had negotiated such places before. He turned the vehicle around and they picked up their former course. They traveled for a good five minutes before the police sergeant spoke.

"You going to tell me?"

Bolan laid out the information he had gained from Stony Man Farm, adding it to all the other data he had on the kidnapping and the subsequent events. Jomo listened in silence until Bolan had finished.

"Everyone in the country knows Chakra is an ambitious man, but I never imagined he would be the one who would betray Karima."

"We haven't exactly caught him with his finger on the trigger," Bolan said. "Maybe we're looking at a covert group within the military."

"Either way doesn't look good for us."

"I won't push you to go on," Bolan said.

Jomo stiffened. "I'll pretend I didn't hear that, Belasko."

"That's what I thought you'd say."

Jomo glanced at him, then grinned. "You're *almost* as smart as me."

"I take that as a compliment."

Jomo was looking ahead. He leaned forward to confirm something he had spotted. "Belasko, let's hope we're both as smart as we think we are," he said.

Bolan checked out what Jomo had seen. They were still a good way off, but there was no mistaking the uniforms, or the weapons, or the military formation of the five-man squad walking in their direction. Behind them was an ACMAT VLRA, a French-built military truck. Behind the driver and his navigator, the open back of the truck had a swivel-mounted 7.62 mm machine gun. Someone shouted an order to the ground troops and they scrambled back inside the truck.

It appeared the pilot of the plane they had encountered had managed to convey their position to his ground squad, and they were moving in to complete the job he had started.

The Land Rover jerked as Jomo slammed on the brakes. He gripped the steering wheel and jammed his foot back on the gas pedal, working through the gears as the vehicle picked up speed.

The harsh rattle of the 7.62 mm machine gun rose over the roar of the motor. The first burst sent rounds into the ground to the left of the Land Rover. Mounds of earth flew in the air, showering Bolan and Jomo.

"Man, is it like this all the time with you?" Jomo yelled above the gunfire.

"No. Sometimes it gets noisy," Bolan answered.

Bolan twisted around in his seat and saw the ACMAT coming up on them fast. The bounce of the vehicle added to the machine gunner's problems as he tried to settle his aim on the Land Rover. This was highlighted by his next burst, which fell disastrously short.

"Nowhere to go out here," Jomo yelled. "Our only cover is to the east. Some low hills. But they might be too far for us to reach."

Bolan had his Uzi cradled in his arms, cocked and ready to fire. He glanced at Jomo, seeing the hard set to the man's face.

"Hit the brakes when you're ready. We take the fight to them. Soon as we stop go EVA. Start shooting once you touch the ground. Don't stop for anything. It's us or them, Jomo, and I don't feel like dying in Africa."

Jomo laughed. "Me neither. Well, not for some time yet."

He made sure his carbine was close at hand, glanced at Bolan, then took his foot off the gas pedal and hit the brake. The Land Rover sideslipped, swinging part way around as it slowed. Jomo cut the motor, took hold of his autorifle and swung himself out of his seat.

Bolan hit the ground and turned to face the oncoming ACMAT. His Uzi came on track, his finger stroking the trigger. A stream of 9 mm slugs arced toward the truck, the first burst shattering the windshield. Glass fragments blew into the faces of the driver and the man alongside him. They arched back, clawing at their bloody faces and the Executioner's second burst took them out of the picture for good. Bolan ran forward, moving in a semicurve that brought him alongside the ACMAT as it came to a juddering stop, stalling as the engine died. Bolan swept the rear of the truck, spinning the machine gunner away from his weapon, his upper torso torn and bloody as the 9 mm rounds impacted his flesh.

Jomo's carbine, set for single shots, cracked with methodical precision. He took out three of the opposition with three shots, moving in on the truck as he fired. Before each shot he paused, fired, then moved again until the next shot.

As the truck's last two occupants scrambled from the vehicle, firing on the move, they encountered Bolan on one side and Jomo on the other. Return fire was ragged and poorly aimed. The opposition had been caught off guard.

One of the men from the truck dropped to his knees beside one of his fallen companions. Briefly covered, he swung his SA-80 on line and triggered a short burst in Jomo's direction. Jomo stepped back and stumbled. Aware that he made a hit, the shooter started to rise, finger still on the trigger. He took the maneuver no further. Bolan, coming up from behind the truck, caught him with a burst that blasted through the man's body, shattering ribs and erupting out of his chest in a spatter of bloody debris.

The last man dodged behind the truck, down on his knees, searching for a clear shot. In the confusion he had forgotten Jomo was still on his feet. He remembered when a shadow fell across him. He twisted, only just seeing the muzzle of Jomo's weapon before it fired into his body, slamming him to the ground. The policeman fired again, a final shot to the head.

Bolan checked the truck for signs of life. There were none. He moved by the bodies on the ground, removing weapons from possible use out of habit.

Jomo was on his knees, muttering through clenched teeth.

His right hand was clamped over his side, blood seeping heavily between his fingers. He glanced up as Bolan approached.

"You ever been shot?" he asked the American. Bolan nodded and Jomo said, "Man, it bloody hurts."

Bolan took a look at the wound. There was a bullet hole, weeping blood. There was no way of knowing how deep the slug had gone.

"Can you move?"

Jomo looked at him. "Why?"

Bolan was staring over Jomo's shoulder. "Because these guys have a backup team."

Jomo followed Bolan's finger. A second ACMAT was heading in their direction from the south.

"You want to drive?" Jomo asked as he and Bolan returned to the Land Rover.

Bolan climbed behind the wheel and started the engine. He dropped the vehicle in gear and moved off. "Any ideas?"

Jomo had been scanning the surrounding terrain. He eased forward in his seat then nodded. He indicated a range of low, stony hills to the east. They were a way off, but appeared to offer the only chance for cover.

"Remember when I said they were too far away? Looks like we're going to find out just how far," he said.

6

"No point giving them the benefit of the doubt?" Jomo asked, fingering his autofire. "Personally I wouldn't."

"Evasion seems to be the word that springs to mind," Bolan said.

"At least it's a compromise."

Bolan hauled the Land Rover in a tight half circle and slammed the gas pedal. He worked through the gears quickly, accelerating with as much speed as he could coax from the vehicle. Land Rovers were built for endurance and all-terrain travel, not for claiming land speed records. Bolan pushed the vehicle to its limit, the SUV picking up speed with what seemed agonizing slowness.

Checking their back trail, Bolan saw the ACMAT take up the pursuit, dust clouding behind them.

"If we can stay ahead and reach those hills," Jomo yelled above the rattle of the Land Rover's diesel engine, "at least we'll have some cover."

The chatter of automatic fire preceded streams of 7.62 mm bullets gouging the ground behind and to the left of the Land Rover. Bolan peered back over his shoulder and made out a figure behind the machine gun mounted on the pursuit vehicle. It looked to have the same specification as the other ACMAT they had encountered. Again accurate fire was difficult as the gunner was unable to control the sway of the weapon. There was always the chance that he might get lucky and lay some of his fire into the Land Rover, Bolan thought.

The range of low hills was getting closer. The soldier tried coaxing a little more speed from the Land Rover. The terrain began to get rougher as they neared the lower slopes. The hill range was mostly bare rock, with a scattering of vegetation dotted across the undulating slopes. Jomo directed him toward a particular section, so Bolan guessed the man knew a place that would help to conceal them.

Whatever Jomo's intention, Bolan never found out.

He felt the Land Rover judder as 7.62 mm fire chewed into the rear of the body. Shards of aluminum sprayed the interior of the vehicle, smacking against the legs of his blacksuit. More autofire followed and this time the hot projectiles cored through one of the rear tires, shredding rubber. The tire blew and the Land Rover lurched out of control. Bolan struggled with the wheel.

"Time to leave, Jomo," Bolan yelled. "Get out."

The stricken Land Rover hit a projecting rock and shook violently, the floor under Bolan lifting him in a slow-motion tilt. He clung to the Uzi and pushed himself over the side of the Land Rover as it started to roll. Bolan was flung away from the vehicle. He landed on his feet, his forward motion carrying him away from the somersaulting vehicle. He tried to stay upright but his body weight overcame him and he crashed to the ground, rolling and bouncing for yards before he was able to stop. Rough stone scraped the side of his face, leaving stinging flesh in its wake. He felt a stab of pain in his left hip as he slammed against something sharp and unyielding. The moment he had himself back under control, Bolan pushed to his feet. Over his shoulder he saw the SUV coming down in its final moments. It hit the ground on its back, wheels still spinning and engine howling. The impact tore the vehicle apart, scattering debris in every direction.

"Belasko!"

Bolan glanced around and saw Jomo, his face and head bloody, waving at him. The African still carried his SA-80 carbine. Jomo indicated a jumble of boulders. They comprised different shapes and sizes, and looked to be spread for some distance. Bolan followed Jomo and they pushed into the midst of the boulders.

The sound of the pursuit vehicle reached their ears. Brakes squealed as the vehicle ground to a halt. Shouted commands followed. Then came the thump of boots on the hard ground and the rattle of weapons.

"Keep moving," Bolan said to Jomo.

They wound between the wind-scoured rocks, dust rising in their wake, marking their position.

A weapon fired. The bullet struck rock off to their left, leaving a score mark in the surface. More shots came, peppering the rocks around Bolan and Jomo. Dust and stone fragments misted the air with each hit.

Bolan heard Jomo gasp. He looked round and saw the African was on his knees, clutching his wounded side. He was cursing in a low voice.

"Get out of here, man. Do what you came for. I'll hold these bastards off."

Bolan shook his head. He bent over Jomo to help him up.

The policeman reached out with his free hand and pushed the American aside.

"Don't be a bloody fool, Belasko. What are you going to do? Carry me?"

The random shots were getting closer.

"No point both of us dying here, man. Go on, get out of here. If I lose them maybe we can join up later. If I can hold them off it gives you a chance."

Jomo held up his carbine. He used it to push himself upright, propping himself against a slab of rock. "Go now, Belasko. Don't let these bastards run Karima out of office. Find his kids and get them home. Give the man his chance."

The gunfire increased, showering Bolan and Jomo with stone chips. Jomo hunched and laid his carbine in a fissure, aiming and firing. A man yelled in pain.

"Get out of here," Jomo said.

Bolan backed off. He was aware of the sacrifice Jomo was making, buying the Executioner time to slip away. Bolan pushed his way through the maze of rock, listening to the steady crack of Jomo's weapon. The only way he could repay Jomo's sacrifice was by doing exactly what he came to Tempala for. From this moment on he was committed to that end. If not for Karima, then it had to be for Christopher Jomo.

Bolan dropped to his knees and crawled beneath a rocky overhang. The sound of the gunfire was fading behind him. He could still pick out the singular crack of Jomo's carbine. The overhang led him down a dusty runoff, created by draining water. Bolan reached the bottom and found himself in a shallow basin worn from the rock. The basin had no water in it, only a layer of gritty dust. He checked the area. It appeared that the way in was also the way out. Bolan worked his way around the enclosure. The rocks that formed the sides and top of the basin were tightly packed. He almost missed the narrow fissure in the rocks. There was enough of a gap to let him crawl through. He eased into the fissure and worked his way along the confining tunnel. It curved off to the right, the ground under him sloping down. As it did, the tunnel widened a little and the roof over his head became higher. Bolan kept moving, trying not to dwell on the notion that if the tunnel dead-ended he would have to make a return journey.

The sound of the gunfire had almost faded. Bolan was in near silence. The only sound was him crawling along the gloomy tunnel. But at least he wasn't in total darkness. There was light filtering through from somewhere, thin shafts that pushed back the shadows and allowed him a degree of guidance. He realized that the light source was becoming stronger the farther he moved.

Bolan felt the ground under his hands drop away sharply. He eased back, peering ahead. The tunnel floor had become a steep slope that led into a hollow deeper than the basin he had found earlier. And there was more light here. Dusty shafts, alive with dust particles, swirled in front of him. Bright light beamed through cracks and gaps in the clusters of stone above his head. He checked out the area. To his left he saw a chimney of rock a good six feet wide, angling up toward the main light source, and when he tilted his head he caught a glimpse of blue sky, only a sliver showing through the rocks twenty or so feet above his head.

The sound of gunfire had receded as he negotiated his way deep into the rocks. Now there was nothing.

How did he interpret that?

Was Jomo dead?

Taken prisoner?

He could have spent a lot of time deliberating, but Bolan's priority was survival, pure and simple. The mission had become something entirely different from the one he had started out on. Conditions had changed. There were complications that added to the picture as a whole. Bolan would deal with them, in his own way and in his own time. Right now he needed to stay alive, because if he didn't it wouldn't matter how complicated the plot became.

He propped the Uzi against a rock, unclipped and removed his combat harness. He assessed his ammo supply, replenishing the Uzi first. With that done he peeled off the blacksuit and examined the wound on his hip. There was a jagged tear in the outer skin that had bled but had congealed now. Bolan decided it wasn't as bad as he had first suspected. And there wasn't a great deal he could do about it in his current situation. There was a small medical kit in the bag that had been lost when Jomo's Land Rover had crashed. If the search squad moved on he might be able to recover his gear. If not, the wound would have to remain unattended.

As Bolan pulled the blacksuit back in place he found his thoughts returning to Jomo. The policeman had still been firing on the attackers the last Bolan had seen of him. The firing had ceased since then. The soldier asked himself again—was Jomo dead? Was he in the hands of the enemy? Neither option gave Bolan any comfort. He felt responsible for Jomo. Despite his commitment to the mission he refused to push Jomo from his mind. The man had willingly joined up with Bolan once he had been made aware of the situation, and he had been a good partner in the short time they had been together. Whatever else Bolan had on his agenda, finding out what had happened to Jomo was now added.

Bolan remembered his cell phone. He reached to unzip the pocket where he had placed the phone. The moment his fingers brushed the material of the pocket he knew the worst. The cell phone had taken a heavy blow sometime during the last couple of hours. Maybe when Bolan had been thrown from the overturning Land Rover. He took it out. The phone was badly damaged. The screen had been shattered and the body of the phone was cracked. Bolan pressed the power button. Nothing happened. When he slipped the power pack from the phone he saw that it, too, had been damaged. He replaced the power pack and tried once again, unsuccessfully, to switch on the phone. It remained dark and lifeless. Bolan made certain he had removed the SIM chip from the phone before he abandoned it. He broke the small memory card into small pieces and scattered them.

Bolan examined his other weapons, making sure they were both fully loaded. He glanced at his watch. At least another two, maybe three hours before dark. No point moving before then. If the squad was still around, emerging in broad daylight would make Bolan an easy target. The night would cloak his movements, offer him a better chance to locate the enemy.

He considered that point. The men who had attacked him and Jomo had done so without provocation. They had identified their quarry and had gone in for the kill without hesitation. No challenge. No attempt at mediation. They had gone for the throat like ravaging dogs.

Bolan leaned against the rock at his back, staring at the wall of stone opposite. The rules had been laid down. So be it. The Executioner would respond in kind. He had no choice. He'd fight back or allow himself to become a victim. That was something Bolan had never done in the past, never even considered. He would never be a victim. It wasn't in his nature to stand meekly by and let that happen.

He settled against the rock and relaxed. Waiting was his only option so he might as well try to rest.

7

The penetrating rays of the sun had disappeared when Mack Bolan opened his eyes again. There was little light showing in his den. Bolan reached for the Uzi and slung it across his back. He moved to the chimney of rock and started to climb. The interlocked chinks of rock made the ascent easy. There were ample hand and foot holds. Bolan climbed steadily, keeping the sound level as low as possible in case any of the opposition were still within earshot. As he neared the top of the chimney he felt a coolness in the air. When he emerged into the open there was a soft, cool breeze drifting in from the west. Bolan pulled himself clear and crouched in the shadows while he checked out the lay of the land. He was at a point higher than where he had first crawled into the rocks, able to look down on the spot where he and Jomo had taken cover. The sun had almost set but there was still enough light for Bolan to see.

There was no sign of the African. Until he knew otherwise Bolan took it as a good sign. Maybe Jomo had managed to give the enemy the slip after all.

Bolan worked his way down the rocks until he was back

where he had started. He could see marks in the dust where he and Jomo had stood. There were empty shell casings littering the ground. The soldier picked one up and examined it. It was 5.56 mm, the kind Jomo's SA-80 carbine used.

He heard little to alert him apart from the regular wildlife. No smells that might suggest a cookfire or someone smoking. Despite the lack of those things Bolan remained wary. Complacency could be a man's undoing. Just because things seemed right didn't make them right.

His caution was rewarded when he picked up the merest whisper of a footstep on loose earth, the disturbance of gritty dust as someone moved. Bolan sourced the sound, easing in that direction. He stayed well back in the cover of the rocks while he checked out the immediate area. He was looking for shadows, for something, anything, that would show him where the creator of the noise had come from.

His patience was rewarded when a uniformed figure stepped into view. The man was armed with a standard SA-80 rifle and carried a sheathed panga knife. The man held a compact transceiver to his mouth and was talking softly as he moved. He halted directly in front of Bolan's place of concealment as he continued to speak into his transceiver. The man wasn't speaking English so Bolan had no idea what he was saying.

The content didn't matter all that much to the Executioner right then. He was more interested in moving in on the trigger-happy group that had attacked him and Jomo. Bolan wasn't about to forget—or forgive them. He hadn't expected his mission in Tempala to be any kind of picnic, but the savage dedication the assault group had put into their attack had only succeeded in bringing out Bolan's obstinate character.

He didn't take to being pushed to the edge and not be expected to push back.

Right now he was in extreme push mode. And that meant trouble for the ones who had set the agenda for this particular confrontation.

Bolan waited until the man moved on, clipping the transceiver back on his belt. Once the dark figure had rounded a jutting mound of rocks, Bolan eased into the open and followed. Staying well in the deep shadows, he had lost sight of the soldier, but could still hear the soft footsteps as the man crossed over loose gravel and gritty sand. Rounding the rock outcrop Bolan picked up a soft glow of light ahead. He held back, scanning the area and saw a campsite. Out in the open a fire burned in a shallow pit. The Executioner could see three seated figures. The man he had followed was making his way across the open ground. He joined his three companions as they sat talking, drinking coffee from a steaming metal can suspended over the fire on a metal tripod. Just beyond them was the dark outline of the ACMAT. Behind the truck was a wide, shallow stream and a short distance farther the ground rose in an uneven slope.

Bolan studied the layout of the camp. The four men had done little to create any kind of perimeter defense. From the way they acted he figured there couldn't be many more of them, if any. He stayed where he was for almost fifteen minutes, watching and also checking out the rocks and the dark terrain beyond the truck. Nothing else showed or moved.

Four to deal with.

Bolan decided to work his way around to the rear of the truck and check that in case there were any off-duty members of the group asleep in the vehicle. It could have been an easy matter to overlook the truck. An easy mistake that could have fatal results.

He slipped back into the deep shadow, starting out in a wide circle that took him beyond the vision of anyone in the camp. Bolan moved steadily, the Uzi ready in his hands. He kept the camp and the four men in his sight the whole time. It took him almost thirty minutes to reach the rear of the truck. He dropped to his knees, easing the Desert Eagle from its holster.

Moving along beside the truck, Bolan's eye was attracted by something fluttering. He turned his head—and saw Christopher Jomo's SA-80 carbine leaning against the rear of the cab. The bright feathers fastened to the stock were moving in the night breeze.

Bolan also saw the dark patches of dried blood marking the weapon. There was no way Jomo would have given up his weapon unless he had been captured—or worse.

He fixed the image in his mind as he continued to the front corner of the truck, from where he could see the four men clustered around the cook fire.

Bolan raised the Desert Eagle and selected his first target, firing the moment he had acquisition.

The .44 Magnum round cored the back of the target's skull, mushrooming out between his eyes, shoving him forward. He toppled over the fire pit, his body smothering the flames. The steaming coffee spilled from its pot and was turned to hissing steam by the red hot embers of the fire.

The remaining three dropped their mugs and reached for the weapons they had beside them, pushing to their feet and turning to seek the sniper.

Bolan's Desert Eagle snapped a second and a third time.

One man went down howling, a bullet deep in his chest.

Number three was caught on the turn, the round gouging out his throat. He tumbled, coordination all gone. He hit the ground, squealing in hurt and fear, hands tight over the ragged wound pumping gouts of blood.

The last man standing snatched up his weapon and took a long, lunging stride away from the area, hoping to lose himself in the twilight. Bolan hit him on the run, his bullet clipping the man's hip and knocking him off his feet.

Moving quickly, Bolan took weapons and additional ammunition from the bodies. He also took possession of all the transceivers the men had been carrying. He carried them all to the truck and dropped them inside. He crossed to the shot man, taking hold of his SA-80 rifle. He frisked the man and relieved him of a knife. The rifle and knife, plus the man's transceiver also went into the truck.

Bending over the moaning figure Bolan took a firm grip on the man's tunic and hauled him across to the truck where he slammed the rebel against one of the wheels. The man stared up at the Executioner, eyes blazing with defiance. The moment he slid to the ground he kicked out at Bolan and rolled, scrambling to his feet. He was agile, fit, and he regained his footing in seconds despite the hip wound. As Bolan went after him the man spun, driving a hard snap kick that was aimed for the Executioner's face. Bolan, swinging his right arm up to knock his opponent's leg aside, followed up with a kick of his own. The sole of his boot cracked against the African's left knee, hard enough to draw a grunt of pain from the man. Before the man could regain his balance, Bolan moved in close, driving a solid left fist against the gunman's jaw. Something cracked and the man grunted, spitting blood. The rebel recovered fast, ducking low and aiming for Bolan's mid-section. He slammed into the Executioner, spinning them both off balance. They hit the ground, Bolan underneath his adversary.

They both struggled to gain the upper hand, the only sound coming from them was the exhaling of breath. Bolan wriggled a hand between their bodies and caught hold of the man's collar. He made a powerful lunge, rolling the African off him, bringing his own body over and on top. Still gripping the collar, Bolan pulled hard, tightening his grip, and the edge of his hand pressed into the man's throat, closing off his air supply. The man began to struggle, choking. The Executioner gripped even tighter and the rebel began to thrash about. He was gasping for breath, his hands clawing at Bolan. Getting his feet under him, Bolan hauled the man off the ground, turning him so they were face to face.

The man made a final, weak attempt at resistance. His effort made little difference to the outcome as Bolan yanked him in close, then used the palm of his hand to strike under the jaw. The man flew backward, arms flailing, control lost. He stumbled and fell, landing hard. He lay in a dazed stupor, the world spinning before his eyes, and when the dizziness faded and he could see again he was looking down the barrel of Bolan's Desert Eagle.

"Your choice, pal. We can play this game all day if you want or you can answer my questions and stay alive. Your choice."

The man touched his hand to his bleeding mouth, staring at the blood staining his fingers. He rolled something around in his mouth before spitting out pieces of a broken tooth. "Man, you broke my fucking tooth."

Bolan ignored the man's complaint. He simply pushed

the Desert Eagle closer, the muzzle almost touching the man's cheek.

"You're wasting the time you have left. I suggest you think about what you say next. The way things have been going the last couple of days have left me a bit touchy. Understand what I mean?"

The man looked into the big American's eyes and what he saw must have scared him. Bolan's eyes were ice blue, startling in their intensity. There was a warning in the steady, unflinching stare that told the rebel he was as close to death as he ever could be and remain alive.

"What the hell do you want to know?"

"Where are Karima's children? And don't insult me by saying you don't know what I'm talking about. Your team took them from their car, murdered the driver and set off for the bush with the children. I want to know where you've got them."

The rebel dabbed at his bloody mouth again. Blood was running down his chin and dripping onto his khaki shirt. He pressed a hand to the hip wound, staring at the blood oozing between his fingers.

"Man, I could bleed to death here."

"You could also catch a bullet in the head. You choose."

"You're too late. We don't have them any longer."

"What did you do? Send them home? Kill them?"

The rebel shook his head, blood spraying from his face.

"You don't understand, man. We don't have them because they were taken from us."

"Make it clear, pal, I can't keep my finger off this trigger for much longer."

"The team with the children was hit by slave traders. They

came out of nowhere and took them by surprise. They killed most of the team, then they took all their food and water. And their weapons. The report said the slavers took Karima's kids as well. Put them in chains and added them to their collection. They had about forty, maybe fifty already. Women and kids as well as men."

Bolan stared at the rebel. The man was telling him the truth. Had to be. His story was too clever to have been made up. Something else clicked in Bolan's brain. Something that made sense now.

"That's why you set off the bomb in Tempala City. Losing the children means you've lost your bargaining chips. No kids, no deal. Sooner or later you would have to show the president you still had his kids alive and well. Once they were taken from you everything changed, so you decided to bring the deadline forward by adding pressure."

The rebel refused to look him in the eye this time. Bolan had hit the jackpot. The rebels had lost the kidnapped children to a bunch of wandering slave traders. It was almost enough to make him laugh. The trouble was this new twist only made his mission potentially more difficult. Tracking the rebels had been hard enough. Now he was going to have to start over and set out to locate the slave traders who had snatched Karima's kids from the rebels.

"Which way did they go? The traders. Don't think about it, man. Tell me."

The rebel waved a bloody hand beyond Bolan. "I guess to the west. For the coast. Meeting their ship."

The rebel slumped back against the ground, hands clutched to his battered face. He was not going to offer any kind of resistance to Bolan.

"One more question. The man who was with me? Where is he?"

The rebel didn't answer until Bolan nudged him with his boot.

"They took him back to our base."

"He's alive?"

"He was when he left here."

Bolan crossed to the ACMAT and located a folded map. He returned and pushed it under the rebel's nose. "Where?"

The rebel stared at the map. He unfolded it and spread it so the moonlight illuminated the contours of the area printed on the sheet. He pressed a finger to a pencilled square. "That's it."

"Where are we right now?" Bolan snapped.

The finger moved to indicate a spot.

"That uniform you're wearing? It has the insignia of the Tempala military on it. Has the army gone over to the rebel side as well?"

"What if we have? Karima's going to get a surprise soon."

"I just like to know exactly who I'm dealing with," Bolan said, standing up and walking back from the man.

"Why? You figure you can do something about it?"

Bolan let the Desert Eagle answer for him. "Something like that," he said to the dead rebel.

The Executioner took the map and made his way to the ACMAT. The key was in the ignition. Bolan climbed in. He started the engine and eased the ACMAT into gear, turning it west. He drove across the stream and up the slope that lay on the far side. At the top Bolan braked and sat staring out the windshield. He checked the compass mounted on the dashboard. He was heading west. He took another look at the map, checking his position. From that he was able to mark his route to the coast. The map showed any number of likely places the traders might be aiming for. The river Jomo had mentioned showed on the map. It meandered across the plain until it ran into the ocean. The coastline would offer numerous quiet bays and inlets where a ship could come in close to shore, take on passengers and be gone before anyone noticed. Bolan doubted the country had a sophisticated coast guard service, so any illegal entry into the offshore waters would most likely go unchallenged. Which meant Bolan was going to have to run his own interference on this one.

He set off again, driving at a steady pace while he tried to figure out where the slave traders were heading. Some input from Stony Man Farm and Kurtzman's satellite imaging would have been useful, but Bolan's cell phone was long gone. Unless he could find some way of contacting the Farm he was going to have to depend on his own skills, and maybe a strong helping of good luck.

He hadn't asked the rebel if there was any communication equipment at the base. He was banking on the answer being yes to that question. If there was it might enable him to contact Stony Man and have Kurtzman make a satellite sweep. If they hit lucky the computer expert might be able to pick up the slavers and their captives. It was a long shot but it was worth considering. It had to be better than nothing, which was the sum total of Bolan's information right now. Sure, he knew the slavers were heading west. That left him with a hell of a chunk of land to check out, and the longer he spent doing that the more time the slavers had to reach their rendezvous.

There was no way the soldier could calculate how many of the enemy he might find at the rebel base, either. A few, or maybe a hundred. In his current frame of mind Bolan didn't give a damn. However many were there he would find some way of dealing with them. He also needed to locate Christopher Jomo. And if there was some form of communication setup, he was going to use it come hell or high water.

8

Christopher Jomo's body hurt all over. There didn't seem to be a part of him that didn't ache. The bullet wound in his side had already weakened him considerably. When his senses recovered sufficiently for him to assess his position he realized it wasn't good. He was in the hands of a rebel murder squad. That in itself told him his life expectancy had been drastically reduced. These people would have little sympathy for Jomo, particularly because he came from a different tribe than theirs, and in Tempala that was enough to guarantee a hard time at their hands.

With that in mind, the policeman decided to escape at the first opportunity. Any escape attempt would be met with fierce resistance, which he expected, and could easily result in his death. The latter would probably be welcome if he spent much time in the company of these men. Jomo didn't relish the prospect of death, but when he weighed it against the horrors these men could inflict on him, it appeared the lesser of two evils.

Jomo heard someone approaching. He remained where he was, huddled against the side of the building where he had been thrown after refusing to acknowledge their authority.

Hands caught hold of his clothing and he was dragged outside and thrown on the dusty ground. The side of his face struck the ground hard, sending stabs of pain through his head.

"Hey, be careful. This one is a policeman. He'll arrest us."

A general round of laughter followed the words. A hard boot slammed into Jomo's side, over his ribs. He winced against more pain.

"One of Karima's pet officers," someone else said.

A harsher voice yelled at the men to stop wasting time. They hauled Jomo to his feet and manhandled him to an old truck parked in the compound of the base. Rope was used to secure him to the side of the truck, pinning him there helpless.

Jomo faced his captors. There were five of them clustered around him. The one who shouted the orders came and stood in front of Jomo.

"You have killed some of my people," he stated.

"Not enough," Jomo replied, regretting his words the instant he had spoken. "I would have killed more but they ran away."

The rebel even smiled before he struck the sergeant full in the face with the short wooden club he had been holding out of sight. The force of the blow shattered Jomo's left cheek bone, tearing the flesh. Blood began to course down the side of his face, soaking his already dirty shirt. The blow snapped Jomo's head to one side. He let it hang, biting back the moan of pain that he wanted to express. But he refused to make a sound in front of these people.

Slowly raising his head he looked his captor in the eye. "Even now you can only hit me because my hands are tied," Jomo said.

The rebel looked round at his companions. "This one believes he is tough."

The club struck again. Over and over.

Jomo's head and shoulders took the brunt of the attack, and by the time the man had finished, Jomo's head was dripping blood. His face was a glistening bloody mask. His lips were torn and raw, gums and teeth badly damaged.

The rebel looked down at the club in his hand. Blood stained its short length. His hand was bloody, too, and more had spattered the front of his shirt. He was breathing hard, face shiny with sweat.

"Did you think you could stop us? You and your American friend? Just the two of you?"

"And did you and your rebel dogs believe a bomb in the city would frighten the people into submission? You really are as stupid as that. Cowards running around slaughtering because you have no other way to go," Jomo said defiantly.

Jomo's tormentor considered this. He stepped back from Jomo, letting his captive see the bloody club he still carried.

"We asked the people to give us the power to rule the country, but they were so blinded by the things Karima promised that they failed us."

"No. They were not fooled by the way you wanted to control them. They voted against you. They told you no, but you were not men enough to accept that. So you started to kill and intimidate the very people you said you wanted to represent."

"The ones who rule are Karima's kind. The Tempai. They wanted to stay in power so they used their influence to make the election go their way."

"Always the old arguments. The Tempai and the Kirandi. Tribal foolishness that has no part in this day. You stir up tribal feuds and ancient customs to use them to alarm the people."

Jomo's outburst exhausted him and he let his head fall forward onto his chest. He was in extreme pain. His face and head burned from the extent of his injuries, and he was finding it hard to concentrate. His vision was blurring, not helped by the blood that kept running into his eyes.

His captor jammed the tip of the club under Jomo's chin and forced his head up, staring deep into his eyes. "We will win. The Kirandi have always been stronger."

"Only through fear and violence. You have been asked to join with Karima many times, and every time that offer has been thrown back in his face."

"Why should we take what he offers when we can have it all?"

"And end up with a nation in ruin? With nothing to look forward to but more bloodshed and misery? Why deny the people a chance to live a better life?"

"By making bargains with the fucking Americans? By selling the rights to our natural resources?"

"What would *you* do with the copper? Leave it in the ground where it does no one any good? If we negotiate with the Americans and allow them to use the deep-water harbor at Rugendi, look at all the work that will bring, a facility for the copper to be loaded on ships. More work. More money for Tempala."

"We don't need outsiders coming here."

"The old chiefs don't want it. They want Tempala to stay in the past. To cling to old ways that have brought us nothing but poverty and kept this country in the shadows."

"It has kept us strong."

Jomo shook his head. "Heads so deeply stuck in the sand you are unable to see what the future offers. If this is the way you fools want to go then we are all finished."

"At least we will be alive."

Jomo stared at him. "You call this living? The whole bunch of you are as dead as the beliefs you follow. All of you wear the army uniform and call yourselves true Tempalans. Deserters is a better word. You are supposed to protect the people, not betray them."

The group leader spun around on his men, giving orders. The waiting rebels moved forward, past the man with the club, and began to beat Jomo with whatever they had on hand. The savage attack went on for long minutes. Jomo had lapsed into unconsciousness long before it was over.

When it stopped, the lead rebel called off his men. They walked away, leaving only Jomo and the leader. The ground around Jomo was spattered with blood. His clothing was sodden, torn, and the exposed flesh beneath was bruised and cut. The policeman sagged against the ropes binding him, the coils digging into his arms and body. Loose flaps of bloody flesh hung from his battered face. Sometime during the beating the butt of a rifle had been used to crush his fingers against the side of the truck. They hung, bone exposed, at crooked angles.

It was some time before Jomo roused enough to be aware of where he was.

The rebel stepped in close so Jomo would be able to hear what he said. "I want that bastard American who was with you. Where is he?"

Jomo absorbed the question with difficulty. His pain was verging on unacceptable. He knew that his ribs were broken and somewhere in his chest there was a stabbing pain each time he took a breath. This was the worst injury he had ever suffered and Jomo knew he would be lucky to survive.

The rebel repeated his question, this time taking a grip of Jomo's hair and dragging his head up so he could look into his face. Jomo's swollen features had turned his face into a bloated mask.

"You hear me?"

Jomo murmured something between his crushed, bloody lips.

"What?"

Jomo took his time to repeat his words. "He'll come and get you, Kirandi. I'm looking at a dead man. But don't expect me to tell you where he is. I wouldn't want to spoil the surprise when he shows up."

Then he summoned all his strength and spit bloody spittle directly into his tormentor's face.

The rebel stepped back, pawing at the blood on his face. He turned on his heel and strode up to one of his men, snatching the panga sheathed at the man's belt. He returned to where Jomo hung from his ropes, defiant.

"No Tempai does that to me," he screamed. "I was going to kill you quickly but I have changed my mind."

The blade of the panga rose and fell. Soon blood streaked the blade, droplets flying from the tip as the rebel raised it above his head, time after time after time...

9

"One man."

The words hung in the stifling air with a tangible presence. The man who had delivered the short comment remained standing, leaning his hands flat against the top of his desk. He was large and broad, with a powerful build that made him, in his uniform, impressive. Colonel Simon Chakra, military commander of Tempala's armed forces. The recipients facing him, from his unit, stood at attention. Their discomfort might have pleased Chakra. If so he didn't let it show. He waited long enough for the silence to become uncomfortable before he spoke again. When he did his tone was soft, a shade off being gentle, but that very restraint threw a chill into the heart of every man standing before him.

"It may have slipped your attention, gentlemen, that we are engaging in a struggle for this country. If we succeed we retain Tempala as it is, and we will then be able to negotiate on our terms. I want Karima out of office. I want his popularity with the people diminished. Right now he is in an extremely strong position. An outright attempt to remove him would not be in our best interests. Which is why kidnapping his children was to be used as a bargaining ploy. I still believe that using Karima's children will achieve what we want. However, that goal has been hampered by the loss of the brats to those damned slave traders. More serious is the involvement of this American, brought in by Ambassador Cartwright. Another example of American interference in our internal business. That said, my chief concern is the plain fact that this American, whoever he is, has managed to run rings around us. The covert squad sent to deal with him has been decimated almost to extinction. And the man is still free."

Chakra paused for effect.

"Am I the only one who views this as something of an embarrassment? One man, on his own, is stopping not only the rebels, but also the Tempalan military. Gentlemen, are you professionals or local militia who run around waving guns and pretending to be real men? I suggest you take time, but not too long, to assess this situation and put it right. Just remember that our role in this has to remain in the background for the time being. Try not to send in a full battalion to capture this man. Use discretion. That will be all, gentlemen. Wait for my orders. Now please get out of my sight."

As the men filed out Chakra sat down, leaning back in the chair to stare up at the ceiling. As the door closed behind the last officer, Chakra turned his head to study the man who had remained silent, standing in a corner of the office, listening to everything Chakra had said.

"I still find it hard to believe," Chakra said. "One man. Right now he's out there looking for Karima's kids and the way he performs he'll most likely snatch them back under the noses of those damn fools I just spoke to."

"Possibly it would be the best thing to happen," Hector

Campos said. "Let this American do all the running and if he succeeds, step in and take the children back."

"Hector, you realize he's working directly for Karima. Probably has a direct line to that bloody misfit."

"Not a nice way to talk about your president."

"The man is a Tempai. That damned tribe has never been anything but a problem. The sooner they are pushed back into the bush, the better. We should be running the country. The Kirandi have always been intellectually superior. It's time we assumed control."

"But as always the problem is the Tempai," Chakra's visitor said. "There are more of them. They have the wealth and the political power. And they have the support of the people. A difficult combination to subjugate."

"If Karima steps down the resistance will weaken. I can promise you that."

Campos stepped up to Chakra's desk. He was lean and dark, with black hair brushed away from his high forehead. He wore a soft white suit and carried a wide-brimmed straw hat in his slender, long-fingered hands.

"I understand your need for caution, Simon. But in the end there has to be a degree of determination that overrides all other considerations." The Cuban advisor smiled. "In simple terms I am telling you that whatever needs to be done, must be done."

"I understood you the first time," Chakra said. "And I will do what is necessary."

Campos reached inside his jacket and drew out a couple of long, thick cigars. He held one out to Chakra. The African took it and bit off the end, watching with amusement as the Cuban carefully trimmed the end of his cigar with a small, sharp knife. After they had lit the cigars Campos sat down.

"This American," Campos said. "He may be known to my people back in Cuba. I will check with my contacts and see if I can find anything."

"So, who do you think he is? Some Yankee mercenary who does work for the American government?"

Campos shook his head. "No. This man seems very different, and not one to dismiss lightly. He is a specialist in his chosen profession. More than a specialist even. More like a man with a mission. Simon, believe me. This is a man to be watched."

"I prefer to look at him as a man who needs eliminating," Chakra said.

"I agree. Consider my earlier suggestion, Simon. Why not let him run. Allow him to track down these slavers and deal with them. Believe me, if this man is a specialist, those slavers are in for a nasty shock. Our mystery American has a perceived sense of moral justice. The taking of children especially will drive him to succeed. Take my word for it."

"If he's that good perhaps I should find him and negotiate a contract. If I have him on my side we'll win easily."

Campos smiled. "No offense, Simon, but you are on the wrong side of the fence as far as this man is concerned."

"Hector, we need to discuss the bomb incident," Chakra said. "If I had Zimbala and Harruri here right now I would execute them on the spot."

Campos raised his hands in frustration. "What can I say? It was a stupid move carried out in panic. When they heard about the children being taken by the slavers they saw the whole scheme falling apart. They acted without due consideration of the consequences."

"Damn right they didn't think about the consequences. An

act like that is only going make us look like savages, and Karima takes a step closer to sainthood. Did you see the video footage of him walking among the debris, talking to the wounded? He did everything except fall on his knees and weep."

"Simon, you are a dyed-in-the-wool cynic."

"My God, we couldn't have given him better publicity if we had actually staged the whole thing. Something like that is beyond price."

Chakra slammed a huge fist down on his desk. "If you see those bloody rebels make sure they stay out of my sight. With dung beetles like that on my side I don't need enemies, Hector."

"I agree they need talking to," Campos said. "We still need their support, Simon. Don't forget you don't have the whole military on your side. If this became a shooting war between your men and Karima's faithful soldiers..."

"I know. On top of everything else, Hector, the last thing I need to be reminded of is that."

"We will talk later. I'm sure you have things to consider on your own." Campos stood and walked to the door. He paused. "Simon, we will achieve what we set out to do. But we must be patient."

Chakra nodded, already deep in thought. He barely heard the door close behind Campos. He sat for a while, toying with the cigar. On impulse he crushed it out in the glass ashtray, then pushed his chair back from the desk. Chakra went and stood at the window, staring out across the flat, dusty parade ground of the isolated training base he was using for his covert operations. He watched a small squad of soldiers being drilled by a ramrod-stiff sergeant-major. The man's hard commands drifted across the parade ground. It was a sound Chakra loved to hear. He had been brought up within earshot of those sounds all his adult life. They were lifeblood to him. The military ethos was as much a part of him as his skin and hair. Simon Chakra was a soldier to the tips of his highly polished combat boots. He watched the drill for a while, losing himself in memories of his own early days in the army. Training under the hot African sun with other eager men who wanted to serve their country. The long days and nights out in the bush, learning their craft, sometimes wondering if they would ever survive. Some of his comrades had not. There had been deaths during those hard months, but with each loss the survivors became more determined to stay the course. Later, after rising through the ranks, Chakra's natural leadership qualities shone brighter than any of his comrades in arms. He was chosen to became an officer. Then the trip to England. Officer training at Sandhurst, where he was tutored in the requirements of the officer class in quiet, oak-paneled rooms and then spent long hours being barked at by ruddy-faced drill sergeants on the parade grounds. The fact he was an officer meant little to the howling monsters who chased Chakra and his friends around the drill grounds. They were treated with contempt, belittled and worked until they were ready to drop. They were denied the satisfaction of responding to the vocal taunts. They took what was thrown at them, staying aloof and letting the abuse wash over them. But at the end of the course each and every man walked out of Sandhurst as an officer, wearing his insignia with pride and knowing he had been schooled by the best. If a soldier could survive Sandhurst, he could survive anything.

Back in his own country Chakra had devoted himself to the business at hand, and years later, when Karima had become president, he had chosen Simon Chakra to command the Tempalan military. As far as Chakra had been concerned there were no others as capable, and he had accepted the position with pride. But that pride had started to fade when Chakra became aware of Karima's weakness—being Tempai—and he allowed his filial loyalty to blur the line between duty to his president and the honor of tribe and country.

Tempala had to be saved from Karima and his kind. They were ready to sell out the country to foreigners, to let in the American military and the greedy U.S. businessmen. If that was allowed to happen, Tempala would become just another U.S. satellite. Chakra wouldn't let that happen. He had to save Tempala from its own folly. If that meant a campaign of enmity with Karima as the target, then so be it. Chakra's alliance with the rebel force had seemed an easy option. Their forces, combined with the army personnel who were on Chakra's team, raised his strength.

Now Chakra was not so sure about the marriage of convenience. The rebels were proving to be an uncontrollable force. Going their own way without consultation and following their own agenda was creating problems. First the kidnapping of Karima's children—a clever enough ploy—had gone wrong when the slave traders had attacked the rebel group holding them. The rebels had been caught unaware, most of the kidnapping team killed and the children taken by the slavers. That had been disastrous enough. Then the rebel leaders had decided to make a point by setting off an explosive device in the city. A bad mistake as far as Chakra was concerned. Stupid and wasteful.

And now there was this damned American running free in the bush causing all kinds of complications.

It was something Chakra didn't need. He wanted things to

be run on military lines. Ordered, planned, with all contingencies considered before anything was done. It wasn't happening. It was time for him to regain control. He had to take hold of the reins again. Quickly. Before the whole matter descended into total chaos.

He would have to conduct the operation himself, which meant stepping out of the shadows and risking being identified with the rebels. That was unfortunate. He had hoped to stay out of sight for as long as possible, maintaining his faith with Karima. That closeness allowed him to learn what was happening within Karima's circle. If he had to take the risk of discovery this early in the game, then that was how it would have to be.

10

The rebel base consisted of a square, flat-roofed building in the center of a low, walled enclosure. The mud-brick construction gleamed dirty white in the morning sun. Parked against the east wall, partially covered by a camouflage net, was a Hummer, painted in olive drab.

Bolan's attention was caught by the two rebels on guard outside the building, the communications satellite dish fixed to the roof—and the motionless figure of a man hanging limply against the ropes holding him to the wooden sides of a beat-up old truck.

The soldier stayed in position for a time, studying the layout and watching to see if there were any other guards. The building itself butted against the east wall, with no more than a few feet of space between building and wall, so there was no likelihood of anyone being concealed there. The compound was open and he had a clear field of vision across the whole area. If there were any others present they were inside the building.

Bolan eased back behind the boulder that concealed him. He was working out his next move. The scene below him presented the Executioner with a number of options. Despite the distance and the blood that seemed to cover the bound man,

Bolan had recognized Christopher Jomo. The policeman looked to be in a bad way. If his injuries were as severe as they appeared from Bolan's standpoint, there was not going to be a great deal Bolan could do for him, no matter how much he wanted to help. However the soldier decided to handle the situation, his first task would be to dispose of the two guards. Then there was the unknown factor. How many—if any— were inside the building? That would reveal itself only when Bolan took on the two guards.

He ran a swift weapons check, making sure each was fully loaded and ready, slinging the Uzi across his chest for easy access. Making his way back to the truck he had left a few hundred yards away, he climbed in and fired up the motor. Bolan dropped it into gear, eased the truck out of the brush and drove around to the west side of the base. He approached the open gate down the long slope that led to it and coasted in that direction.

The guard closest to the gate moved to watch the ACMAT as it came into sight. He recognized the vehicle, leaning forward to stare at the windshield to identify the driver. The dust-streaked glass obscured Bolan's image, giving him a degree of cover. He leaned as far back in the seat as he could, keeping himself away from the screen.

The guard said something to his partner and the second guard started across the compound to join him.

Bolan hung on for as long as he could, then rammed his foot hard on the gas pedal. The truck picked up speed. The Executioner held the wheel steady with his left hand, pulling the strap-hung Uzi into position with his right.

The guards saw the truck hurtling at them and moved to get out of the way.

Mack Bolan stepped on to the running board, leaned out,

then let go. He landed on his feet, caught his balance then executed a shoulder roll. His roll ended when he came up against the base of the wall. Dust from the passing truck boiled around him as Bolan pushed to his feet, the Uzi on track.

The truck struck the opening with its left front fender, smashing through the clay brick construction. It ran on for a few yards before the engine stalled and the vehicle came to a juddering stop.

The first guard skirted the truck, his SA-80 rifle held at hip level. He peered through the dust cloud as he moved around the collapsed section of the wall, seeking the driver of the truck.

Bolan picked out the guard's outline as the man stepped around the wall. He caught the guard with a short burst that punched into the man's chest, throwing him back inside the compound.

The thud of boots on the hard earth told the Executioner the second guard was closing on the truck. Bolan switched sides, moving around the rear of the vehicle. He ran the length of the ACMAT toward the front, catching the second guard unaware. Bolan hit him with another sharp burst, the 9 mm slugs chewing into his body, severing the rebel's spine. The man went down in a loose sprawl, crying out in pain. Bolan laced him with another burst, blowing away the back of the man's skull, silencing him for good.

Bolan cut across the compound, heading directly for the open door of the building. He was ten feet away when an armed man burst through, an autopistol in his right hand. Bolan fired the moment he laid eyes on the man. His Uzi threw a scattering of 9 mm rounds across the man's torso, spinning him and bouncing him off the wall. He crashed to the ground at the base of the wall, kicking in agony as his body reacted to the ravaging effects of the bullets. Bolan fired again as he closed in on the man, the body jerking under the impact, then falling still.

Ejecting the magazine, Bolan reversed it and locked in the fresh one. He cocked the weapon, flattened against the outside wall for a moment before ducking and stepping inside.

The interior comprised a single room. Bolan took in scant furniture and a communications setup at the far end.

He picked up a dark shape off to his right, bending to pick up a weapon leaning against the wall. Bolan raked him with a burst from the Uzi. The impact lifted the hardman and tossed him over the low cot he was standing beside. The cot overturned and fell across the dying rebel.

A shot crashed out. Bolan heard the slug whack into the wall behind him, feeling chunks of clay strike his shoulders. He took evasive action, going down on one knee, and returned fire. The shadowy figure on the far side of the room flew backward, becoming entangled with a chair and fell hard, blood coursing from his chest and throat. He lay for a while choking on blood and sucking in air through his shredded windpipe.

Bolan stayed alert, scanning the room until he was satisfied he was alone. He moved from man to man, checking for signs of life. There were none. He picked up the dropped weapons and threw them in a corner after pulling the magazines. Then he turned and stepped outside, feeling the heat of the sun as he crossed to the old truck—and the figure bound to it.

He heard the harsh buzzing of flies. As he walked around the rear of the truck and came in sight of the bound man, Bolan felt his stomach tighten. He had been right.

It was Jomo.

Or what was left of him.

What Bolan had not been able to see from his previous position overlooking the site were the brutal wounds inflicted on Jomo's body. The mass of congealed blood on the ground around the body attested to the savagery inflicted on the man. His head bore the marks of a prolonged beating. Crusted blood caked his face. His mouth hung open to reveal lacerated gums and broken teeth. One eye had been partially pushed from its socket. That was minor compared to the butchery carried out on the policeman's torso and limbs. A heavy bladed knife, most probably a panga, had been used to chop and slash at Jomo's body, opening deep wounds. A bulge of coiled intestine showed through a deep slash in his stomach. Both hands had been severed at the wrists and his feet cut off at the ankles. The amputated pieces lay on the ground in a crusted pool of dark blood. Jomo had been left to die slowly, bleeding to death from the terrible wounds.

Mack Bolan had seen the worst atrocities man was capable of inflicting on his own species. But his years in the killing grounds had not hardened him to where he was incapable of reacting when he saw such things. In the heat of battle, the Executioner never once stooped to the kind of deliberate cruelty that had been inflicted on Christopher Jomo. He had only known Jomo for a short time, but in that time the policeman had shown his courage and resourcefulness as he and Bolan pursued their enemies. The man had proved to be a warrior, a good and honest man who had been prepared to go that extra mile for something he believed in.

Bolan spent a little time with his friend in mourning for a fallen comrade and silently promised Jomo that he would go that extra mile for both of them.

There would be no turning back.

There would be a closure.

And for the men behind this terrible slaughter there would be no mercy.

Bolan recalled Jomo's reaction to the killing of the children in the bomb explosion back in Tempala City. No mercy.

Bolan took his knife and cut the ropes holding Jomo to the truck. He lowered the body to the ground. Searching the rear of the truck he found some canvas and cut a section out of it to cover Jomo.

This done, the soldier went back inside the building and crossed to the communication gear. He could hear the soft, muted sound of a small generator outside the rear of the building. A thick cable snaked through a small window, connected to the rear of the com set, providing power. The equipment was of French manufacture. It had a digital setup. Bolan quickly scanned the control panel. He clicked the readout to the Stony Man satellite configuration and waited as the roof dish aligned itself. He put on the headset, adjusting the microphone, and as soon as his transmission status appeared Bolan made his call.

HUNTINGTON WETHERS SNAPPED out of his moment of quiet reflection when he picked up Bolan's call. He responded, acknowledging he was receiving loud and clear.

"What can we do for you, Striker?"

"Has there been a satellite scan of the area? Bear was going to run one for me. I need a location."

Kurtzman's deep voice cut in through the transmission. "Where have you been, Striker? We were starting to think you'd gone AWOL."

"Out here? A man would have to be really desperate to quit in this place. Slight operational problems, but I'm getting back on track."

"Listen up," Kurtzman said. "We ran a sweep yesterday. Had some initial high cloud interference but we got through that. Striker, that is one empty chunk of real estate. We worked on what you gave us and we hit lucky near the end of the pass. We spotted a group heading due west. We squeezed the magnification until we could make out a bunch of women, men and kids being pushed along by about nine, maybe ten armed guys. I couldn't swear to it but I'll stick my neck out and say that the bunch under guard were in chains. Striker, you got any charts or maps handy? I can give you some coordinates."

"Give me a minute. There's a mess of stuff here."

Kurtzman waited until Bolan came back on the line.

"Go ahead."

While Kurtzman relayed the map references through to Bolan, Hal Brognola entered the room, Barbara Price on his heels. They listened to the conversation between Kurtzman and Bolan.

"What I need is a rendezvous point," Bolan said. "There's a hell of a coastline to choose from."

Kurtzman beckoned to Wethers. "Take a look at the images we recorded," he said. "Didn't we see a small village right on the beach? Looked deserted to me. But it was in some bay."

"I'll check it out," Wethers responded.

Brognola put on a spare headset. "Striker, how's it looking out there? You identified any of the players?"

"No proof other than a hunch and the information the Bear came up with on Simon Chakra. It appears he's running with a suspect crowd."

"Hector Campos?"

"The same."

"We just had some intel on Campos. Seems he took a flight out of Cuba a couple of days ago. Be interesting if he turns up in Tempala."

"I've been having some run-ins with a covert military unit out here. These guys may be part of the Tempala military operating as a separate unit. They play hard and don't take prisoners."

"Striker, you okay?" Price asked through her headset, sensing something in Bolan's voice.

"I just lost an ally. A good man who didn't deserve to die the way he did."

Price glanced at the others, then spoke again. Her tone was low, the words directed at Bolan alone. "Hey, you go easy there, Striker. People here want to know you're hanging on."

"Thanks. I'm fine."

Kurtzman cleared his throat.

"Got that location for you, Striker."

"Ready when you are."

As Wethers read the information Bolan marked the coordinates on the map. "Anything else I should know about?"

"We spotted a small airfield. Looks like a dirt landing strip. Couple of small huts. Couple of vehicles and an aircraft," Kurtzman said.

"Could you identify it?"

"We ran it through the system and the database picked it out as an EMB-312 Tucano. That any help?"

"I had a run-in with one earlier. Scratched its pride a little before it left. Give me the location of that base."

"It isn't far off your line of travel, Striker." Kurtzman paused. "You thinking of making a house call?"

"Let's say I'll sleep better if it can't come after me again."

Kurtzman chuckled. "Oh, we came up zero on the cell phone. Can't find anything. So I guess we cancel that out."

"Thanks for that," Bolan said. "Too much to expect every inquiry to pay off."

MACK BOLAN SHUT DOWN the transmission and placed the headset on the table. He studied the map and the location points he'd pencilled in. The coordinates Wethers had given him ran roughly in the direction Jomo had outlined to the Executioner. They also fell in line with what the wounded rebel told him. If the slavers stayed on course they would reach the river Jomo had mentioned and that would take them all the way to the ocean. Satisfied, he folded the map and placed it in one of the zippered pockets of his blacksuit. Turning from the table he checked out the room. He located a military-style knapsack and tipped the contents on the floor, going through them, selecting and discarding. Moving around the room Bolan picked up a few cans of field rations and some dry crackers. He found water in plastic bottles floating in a large clay pot suspended from the ceiling by one of the windows. He broke the seal on one and took a cautious drink. The water was surprisingly cool. He dropped a number of the bottles in the knapsack. Crossing the room he spotted a pair of heavy-duty binoculars hanging by a cord from a wooden peg in the wall. Bolan reached up and took the field glasses down, checking them. They were battered and well used, but functional. He draped them around his neck as he moved on.

In a corner he found a small supply of munitions. Loaded magazines for SA-80 rifles, grenades and a box of 9 mm cartridges. Bolan turned and walked back outside to where the Hummer was parked against the east wall of the compound. He dragged off the camou net and sat in the driver's seat.

There was a radio communications unit fitted between the front seats. Bolan stared at it for a moment, then decided he would use it only when the situation really called for it. Once he broke his silence any transmission could be picked up by the opposition. When he tried the starter the Hummer burst into life. He checked the fuel gauge and saw it was full. There were extra cans of diesel fuel strapped in the rear of the vehicle. There was a roof-mounted 7.62 mm machine gun in place. Extra boxes of ammunition for the machine gun were stacked on the floor inside the vehicle. Bolan drove across the compound and parked at the door to the building. He spent the next few minutes loading as much of the munitions as he thought necessary. He returned to the truck he had arrived in and picked up Jomo's SA-80 carbine and placed it in the Hummer. The knapsack he had filled went on the floor of the passenger side of the vehicle. Back inside the building, Bolan put the radio out of action, making sure that no one would be able to repair the thing in a hurry, if at all.

Returning to the Hummer he turned it around, halting briefly where Christopher Jomo's body lay under the canvas cover.

"Thanks, friend," he said quietly, drove out through the gate and turned the Hummer west.

11

The Hummer was concealed some distance away. Mack Bolan lay prone in the dust, studying the small airstrip through the battered binoculars he had acquired. The landing strip itself was nothing more than a stretch of earth that had been cleared of vegetation and large stones, then leveled to a reasonably smooth surface. Some distance from the landing area were a couple of wooden huts. One had an open frontage, and from what Bolan could see, served as a service and spare-parts hangar. There were wooden crates and oil drums scattered around the frontage. The second hut was for the ground crew who serviced the strip. By its size it probably contained sleeping quarters and somewhere for the men on duty to relax. There was a slender radio mast supported by cables next to the hut. A wind sock fluttered lazily from the top of a wooden pole. Bolan could hear music coming through a speaker fixed to the outside of the main hut.

Bolan had spotted an ACMAT parked between the huts. There was also a small refueling vehicle, the squat tank mounted on the chassis of some unidentifiable truck.

The Tucano stood near the service hut. The canopy was

open and a man in coveralls was busy working inside the cockpit. Two more mechanics had the engine cowling off and had their heads deep inside the engine compartment. Bolan spent a considerable time studying the layout and the number of personnel. He counted two more men. One kept himself slightly apart from the others. He wore flight coveralls and had an autopistol in a shoulder rig under his left shoulder. The other, in tan shirt and pants, had headphones slung around his neck, removing them each time he stepped outside the larger hut. He always stood with the pilot, the pair of them in hurried conversations. Once they completed their discussion the man wearing the headphones returned to the hut.

The pilot seemed on edge. He kept waving his arms at the mechanics, plainly urging them to complete their work on the plane. His outbursts had little effect on the crew. They simply raised their heads to stare at him before returning to their work with little visible urgency.

Bolan had the feeling the pilot wanted to be back in the air as soon as possible so he could either renew his search for the Executioner or look out for the slave traders and Karima's children. Whichever it was, Bolan had no intention of letting the Tucano get off the ground again.

Pulling away from his observation point, Bolan worked his way back to the Hummer. He climbed in and stood behind the swivel-mounted 7.62 mm machine gun. He ran a swift weapons check, making sure the ammunition supply was plentiful. Back down behind the wheel he located the grenades he had acquired and made sure they were accessible. He started the engine and let it tick over while he took out the Desert Eagle and made sure it was ready for use. Slipping it back into its holster Bolan put the Hummer into gear and rolled.

He kept his speed down as he approached so the engine was not on high revs. After coasting around a low swell of earth, Bolan put down his foot and gave the Hummer full power as he worked his way through the gears. The vehicle surged forward, kicking up heavy dust clouds as it swung into the open. Bolan took a wide course that brought him along the actual landing strip, with the Tucano between him and the huts.

By the time the ground crew realized they had an unannounced visitor Bolan was well into his run. The men around the Tucano abandoned their positions, dropping to the ground and racing across to grab the weapons they had leaning against the main hut.

Bolan brought the Hummer to a slithering stop, well in range for the machine gun. He left the engine running as he pushed himself up off the seat and hauled himself behind the machine gun. He swung the muzzle around, slid his finger across the trigger and opened fire the moment he had the stationary aircraft in his sights. The first burst fell slightly short, hitting the ground. Bolan used the bullet gouts to track the weapon in for his second burst, walking the volley up to and then into the Tucano. The outer skin punctured as the bullets chewed their way through. With his target fully acquired Bolan stitched the fuselage from tail to engine, metal and plastic spewing into the air. The canopy, already marked from its previous encounter with Bolan and Jomo, shattered fully. Bolan's continuous burst wrecked the cockpit interior, smashing through the instrumentation. He laid more rounds into the engine compartment, undoing the ground crews' repairs and creating more damage.

Spotting movement behind the plane as the ground crew, now carrying their weapons, attempted to return fire, Bolan dropped the muzzle and raked the area beneath the plane. His burst sent 7.62 mm bullets into the earth, then beyond. One man went down, screaming in agony, his weapon forgotten as he clutched at limbs shredded by Bolan's bullets. He lay on the ground, hands bloody, attempting to stop the gouts of red spurting from his legs, his upper body jerking as Bolan's continuous fire sent more bullets into him.

Gasoline was dribbling from the Tucano's ruptured tanks, pooling on the ground under the aircraft. Bolan let go of the machine gun and reached down to snatch up a couple of grenades. He pulled the first pin and hurled the grenade in the direction of the already-crippled plane. The grenade exploded with a hard blast. The left tip of the Tucano's main wing was removed in the explosion. Bolan's follow-up grenade rolled under the wing, close to the undercarriage, and the blast took off the strut and the wheel. The Tucano sagged earthward, the already-weakened wing splitting midway along its length.

Before the smoke had cleared Bolan was back behind the wheel of the Hummer. He gunned the engine and swung the vehicle in a circle that brought him around the rear of the plane and into view of the huts just as spilled fuel ignited and raced back to the main source. The muffled boom of the explosion was followed by a gush of flame that lifted the plane off the ground for brief seconds, tearing it apart. Burning fuel spread out from the Tucano.

Braking, Bolan snatched Jomo's carbine and exited the Hummer. He ducked low, coming around the swirling mass of fire and smoke, emerging close to the larger of the two huts.

The Tucano's pilot, his pistol in his hand, was shielding his face from the heat, searching for Bolan. He barely had time to register before Bolan put him down with a burst that caught the man in the upper chest and throat. The pilot fell back against the wall of the main hut, clawing at his throat as he coughed up frothy red blood.

Autofire drew Bolan's attention and he ducked and rolled, flattening against the side of the hut. Bullets whacked the earth close by. The Executioner stayed where he was, letting the enemy do the running. The remaining two men from the ground crew came at him in a rush, part of their concentration fixed on avoiding the flames from the burning fuel. Their lack of attention gave Bolan the opportunity to hit them both, placing short bursts into each man before they even had time to bring their weapons on-line. They went down in loose sprawls, one rolling into the fringes of the burning fuel, his clothing igniting as it became soaked in gasoline. He thrashed in silent agony until the fire overwhelmed him.

Bolan leaned the carbine against the wall of the hut and pulled out the Desert Eagle. He held the big cannon two-handed as he moved quickly to the door of the hut. Peering around the frame he let his eyes adjust to the dimmer light of the hut's interior. He could hear a man talking busily. Bolan dropped to a crouch, easing inside and moving to the right of the door, flat against the wall.

As he had guessed, the large hut comprised living quarters as well as a communications center. The section he was in contained cots and personal possessions. A small stove, fed by butane gas, stood against one wall, a blackened water pot bubbling over the flame. To his right, at the far side of the hut, was the communications setup. The man in tan shirt and pants was hunched over his radio, haranguing whoever was on the other end of the link.

With the Desert Eagle hard on the man's back, Bolan

lined up with the wide stripe of sweat that had dampened the man's shirt.

"Hey!" Bolan said. "Time's up, friend. Put down the—"

The hardman stopped talking. He held up his left hand, clutching a microphone handset.

Bolan saw the man's right arm move, curling toward his waist, and knew what was going to happen.

"Don't try!"

His warning fell on deaf ears as the man let go of the microphone, spun on the balls of his feet, his right hand coming into view, with the metal of his pistol gleaming as it swept round.

Bolan's finger stroked the big Desert Eagle's trigger. The heavy sound of the .44 Magnum round filled the hut. The bullet cored into the target's side, ripped its way through and blew out under his left arm in a bloody surge of flesh and fragmented bone. The force threw the man into the radio gear. He bounced off and dropped to the floor, giving a final, convulsive breath before his body reduced itself to a series of shuddering spasms.

Bolan took one look at the radio unit and knew he wasn't going to get much use out of it. His bullet, on its exit, had still maintained enough energy to shatter the front of the set before burying itself deep inside. Already the radio's readouts were fading as the equipment shut down.

Bolan prowled the hut, giving it a quick check. There was nothing more for him. He stepped outside and picked up the SA-80 carbine. He returned to the Hummer and climbed in. Driving around to the rear of the huts, he took a couple of his grenades and tossed them under the chassis of the fuel tanker. Kicking the Hummer into motion Bolan moved away, clearing the area before the grenades exploded, blowing the tank wide open and hurling blazing gasoline over the huts.

Pausing only long enough to check his position and line of travel, Bolan set off again.

Behind him the dead bodies, blazing huts and the still-burning Tucano were all that were left to indicate the airstrip had been visited by the Executioner. Bolan was rolling now, his sights set on a confrontation with the distant slave traders and their captives—especially the ten-year-old children of Joseph Karima.

12

Sergeant Masson prowled the ruins of the airstrip. Smoke still rose into the air, staining the blue African sky with its taint. Masson and his small squad had seen the smoke well before they had arrived. It didn't take them very long to make a full assessment of the situation. The base was destroyed. So was the precious Tucano. The entire complement of men, including the pilot, was dead.

Masson sent out his pair of trackers to pick up the trail left by the vehicle that had come in from the east and had moved on toward the west. Both of his men were Kirandi. They knew the country like the backs of their hands. By the time they returned they would be able to give him all the information he needed.

While he was waiting for them to come back, Masson returned to the Land Rover they had traveled in and reluctantly made radio contact with his base, asking to speak to Colonel Chakra. He wasn't looking forward to it. Chakra had been in a raging temper when he had sent Masson and his squad out to check the airstrip. The last contact Chakra had with the base was a frantic message informing them that the strip was under attack and had almost been destroyed. The transmission had been terminated as the sound of a gunshot echoed through the speaker. After that there was no more contact.

Chakra had ordered a squad out. There was no air transport available at the time. Chakra's helicopter was away on another mission, so Masson, his two trackers and his five-man squad were forced to use one of the Land Rovers. The airstrip lay a good three hours from Chakra's base.

Masson's orders were explicit. The moment he arrived and assessed the condition of the air base, he was to radio back to Chakra and update him.

The radio crackled quietly as Masson waited for the colonel to come to the base communications room. He could feel sweat beading his brow. It wasn't from the heat. He pulled off his cap and sleeved the sweat away.

"Sergeant Masson?"

"Sir."

"Give me your report."

"The airstrip has been destroyed, sir. Both buildings have been burned to the ground. The Tucano as well. Nothing left except the burned-out shell. Five bodies, sir. Ground crew, communications operator and the pilot, sir. All dead, sir."

The silence that followed was even more frightening than Chakra in person. All Masson could hear was the colonel's deep, measured breathing. Masson remained silent, waiting for his orders. He could feel sweat forming again. Beads ran down his face, some creeping into the corner of one eye, stinging wildly. Masson didn't move. In the background he could hear his squad walking about, talking as they carried out the removal of the bodies to the shallow grave they had dug nearby. Right then Masson would rather have been doing that himself.

"Sergeant Masson, I want this Mike Belasko stopped. I don't want to see you back here until you can bring me the head of this man. Do you understand me?"

"Yes, Colonel."

"Did you take extra supplies and ammunition with you?"

"Yes, sir. I anticipated we might have to..."

"A simple yes is all I wanted, Sergeant. Now, have you established which way the American went after he left the strip?"

"Tire tracks show he headed west, sir. I have my two trackers following them. As soon as we finish here I will join up with them."

"Good. Masson, stay with this. And keep me informed of any developments. Understand?"

"Yes, Colonel. We won't let you down."

Masson could visualize the predatory smile curling back Chakra's lips when he spoke.

"I know you won't, Sergeant Masson. Failure is not recognized in standing orders. Is it, Sergeant Masson?"

"No, sir."

"Carry on, Sergeant."

Masson broke the connection and dropped the handset. He switched off the Land Rover's radio, turning to pick up a canteen. He took a long drink, letting himself relax. He admired and respected Chakra, believed in what the man was doing, but there were times when the man scared him. Chakra was a dangerous man. Not as a physical adversary. It was something that came from within Chakra. Masson couldn't exactly put his finger on it because it had no form, no identity. Even so it scared him and Masson always tried to walk a wide circle around Simon Chakra, never letting the man get too close mentally.

Masson pulled a pack of cigarettes from a pocket of his field jacket. He picked one out and lit it, drawing in a lungful of smoke. He savored the sweet taste of the tobacco. He smoked half the cigarette before he felt ready to carry on. Damn Chakra! Masson thought. The man always did this to him when things got difficult. And the way things were going at the moment his pack of cigarettes wasn't going to last very long. Masson tried to recall whether he had brought along extra in his kit. If he ran out he could always pick up some locally made ones from any of the villages they passed. As long as they weren't Tempai settlements. The Tempai made cigarettes that were so weak they weren't fit for women to smoke.

Stepping away from the Land Rover, Masson crossed to where his men were shoveling dirt into the mass grave they had dug.

"Finish quickly," he said. "We have new orders."

"We're not going back, Sergeant?" one of the soldiers asked.

"No, Private Yembo, we are not going back. Colonel Chakra has given us an extra job. We are going to follow this bloody American and deal with him."

"That will be fun," someone muttered.

"I don't think so," one of the others said. "Look what he did here. All on his own."

"Just get this finished so we can leave," Masson snapped. "And stop whining. We're Kirandi. Remember why we are doing this."

"Yes, Sergeant."

Twenty minutes later the Land Rover moved on, leaving the smoking ruins of the airstrip behind. Masson, behind the wheel, followed the tire tracks left by the Hummer being driven by the American.

IT TOOK MASSON an hour to catch up with his trackers. They were still moving, loping easily beside the tracks they were following. They stood by and waited when they recognized the Land Rover. Masson pulled alongside.

"Report," he said.

The lead tracker, a tall, lean man with tribal scars marking his cheeks, raised a skinny arm and indicated the tracks. "He's making for the river. We think the slavers would do the same. If they follow the river it brings them to the coast. Maybe the American has found out where they will meet their ship."

Masson nodded. It was sound enough thinking.

"Yusef, take Hanni with you. Go ahead and see where this man leads you. If he finds the slavers we can deal with all of them. Colonel Chakra wants this American's head delivered to him. If we can do this and bring him Karima's brats as well, the colonel should be well pleased." Masson reached into the Land Rover and picked up a transceiver. He passed it to Yusef. "As soon as you find this man, call. Understand?"

Yusef nodded, his bright eyes fierce with the prospect of a fight ahead. Masson reached out to touch his arm. "Be careful, Yusef. This American, Belasko, he's no fool. Respect the man for his skill in battle. Forget that and he will kill you, too."

Yusef smiled, showing crooked teeth. "I understand, Sergeant Masson. We will find him."

Hanni, the second tracker, raised an arm. He was pointing at the distant dark clouds drifting in from the west. "Storm coming," he said.

Masson checked out the sky, frowning. If Hanni was right they were going to travel directly into the storm. They were still in the rainy season, though there had been a distinct absence of it for the last few weeks. Masson watched the rolling mass of cloud. If the rain did come, dropping with its usual force, any tracks would be washed away quickly.

"Yusef, go now. Before any rain comes. Don't lose the American."

Yusef nodded. He touched Hanni's arm and the pair moved off, their long-legged pace covering the ground easily.

"How do they do it?" one of the men asked. "Run all day and never stop?"

"Their people have always been the best trackers," Masson said. "They learn from the moment they can walk how to keep going without food and water for long periods. When they are young they spend weeks out in the bush. They live off the land. The elders teach them how to find water where no one else can find it and how to run for miles with a mouthful of water and not swallow it until they reach their destination."

"I think I'll stay with my canteen," the man said.

The sergeant shook his head in disappointment. "No strength of character these days."

Masson started the Land Rover and moved off, his eyes fixed on the distant figures of his pair of trackers.

13

Mack Bolan had been watching the clouds gather ahead of him. Even while they were a distance away he felt the cooling wind that preceded them. The breeze brought a degree of moisture with it. Bolan sensed the storm coming—and he was heading directly for it. He had no choice but to carry on.

The terrain had changed around him. There was more vegetation now, stands of trees and thicker bush. He negotiated a range of low hills, then dropped onto an undulating plain that stretched away to the west until it merged with the horizon.

There was more wildlife in this area. Bolan saw a pride of lions in the bush. Antelope skipped in and out of cover, staring at him as he passed before darting away with obvious alarm in their eyes. Nature carried on in its quiet, ordered way, Bolan thought, oblivious to man and his self-destructive obsessions.

It was less than an hour later when the first drops of rain fell, striking the dusty hood of the Hummer, then the windshield. Bolan was thankful the Hummer had a closed-in body. He flicked on the wipers and the blades worked busily to remove the wet sludge caused by the rain soaking the dust that layered the screen. He reduced his speed to give the wipers time to remove all the dust and allow him to see clearly again. As the rain increased, dust spumes misted the air as the droplets struck the layer of surface dust. Within the first few minutes the ground had absorbed the rain and the dust began to turn into mud. Bolan felt the Hummer's wheels lose a little traction and he worked his way through the gears until he found the ratio that gave him back control. Despite the urgency of his trip he accepted that he was going to have to ease off. If he ran into problems and had to abandon the Hummer, continuing on foot was not an option he considered lightly.

Reaching a stretch of stony ground Bolan brought the Hummer to a stop. He unfolded his map and spent some time working out his current position. The river he was aiming for lay some way ahead. It snaked across the landscape, twisting and turning in a series of bends that had it almost doubling back on itself at times. It ran south, then curved around to the west and then again almost north. Bolan's line of travel would bring him to it at a point where it widened out as it flowed south. A narrow tributary angled off to the southeast. Beyond that the river began to curve in an arc that would eventually have it back on its westerly course before emptying into the Atlantic. Somewhere along the isolated stretch of coast lay the bay and the village that were Bolan's destination.

He was aware that the location might not be the correct one, that the slavers and their captives might be making for an entirely different rendezvous point. Bolan didn't allow himself to dwell on that possibility. If he did he would end up all over the landscape, moving wildly from one place to another in the hope he might come across his quarry by accident. Bolan preferred to stay with Kurtzman's suggestion. Stony Man's res-

ident computer genius had a knack for coming up with solid
decisions, based on cumulative assessments, technical solu-
tions and logical evaluations. Kurtzman knew when his decisions were going to place the Stony Man operatives in
possible danger, putting their lives in his hands. The combat
teams had full confidence in his abilities, and that confidence
showed in their complete acceptance of any information he
passed to them.

Bolan put away the map and prepared to move on. He
could feel the impact of the rain against the Hummer's body-
work. In the short time he had been studying the map, the rain-
fall had increased. It was nothing short of a torrential
downpour. The Hummer's wipers were having a hard time
keeping the windshield clear. Bolan brought the vehicle down
the rocky incline and back to level ground. He felt the tires
sink into the muddy earth. He kept his speed at a steady
crawl. He wasn't on a defined trail, simply crossing open
ground that was awash with water. The dry earth had quickly
absorbed what it was capable of and the falling rain was gathering in pools. Dry streams were already starting to fill, the
water quickly reaching the edges of the shallow banks and
overflowing.

If Bolan hadn't been concentrating on the way ahead, his
gaze picking out the safest route, he might have missed the body.

As it was he saw it only at the last moment as the overspill
from a fast-flowing stream disturbed the shape and moved it.
Bolan eased the Hummer to a stop. He sat for a moment
checking out the area. There was nothing in sight. He eased
the Beretta from its holster and climbed out of the Hummer,
feeling the hard impact of the downpour. He was soaked by
the time he reached the body.

It was a child. No more than ten, twelve years old. Face-down in the mud.

Bolan holstered the Beretta. There was no danger from this child. Gentle hands turned over the body, and Bolan watched the rain wash the mask of mud from the thin face of a young boy. He saw immediately that it wasn't one of Karima's children. That fact didn't lessen the impact. Bolan looked on the face of innocence and pity for the victim rose and forced him to catch his breath. He had already seen the marks on the thin wrists where shackles had rubbed the skin raw. The boy's clothing, little more than a thin robe, was soaked and peeled away from his upper body, exposing his lean torso. His ribs were visible beneath the flesh, as were the livid marks left by a thin lash. The wounds were still fresh. The face was piti-fully thin, cheeks hollow, and eyes open. They seemed to be staring into Bolan's.

The forced march had likely been the cause of the child's death. He had been removed by force from his family and sur-roundings, destined for a life of captivity, where he would have been nothing more than cheap labor working in some sweatshop, or endless hard labor, or worse if he had been placed in the hands of some sexual pervert. Torn from familiar things, he would have endured a life of relentless deprivation, his rights cast aside as easily as his lifeless body. Bolan couldn't rid himself of the thought that death was the lesser evil for this child. At peace maybe, but so much had been lost in this unnecessary death.

Bolan picked up the frail corpse and carried it to the cover of some brush. He made a grave of sorts, using heavy stones to cover the boy's body, working tirelessly until he had achieved what he could for the lad's resting place. On his feet Bolan held his hands out so the rain could wash away the mud.

"You bastards," he said. He glanced down at the grave before he moved away. "God keep, son. He might forgive. I won't."

Bolan drove on, finding it hard to erase the image of the dead child from his mind. He thought about the other captives being force-marched by the slavers. He gripped the wheel, his knuckles turning white.

The farther west Bolan drove, the heavier the rain became. The downpour was incredibly powerful. The sheer weight of falling rain rocked the Hummer and, despite keeping his speed down, Bolan felt he might soon be in trouble. The Hummer was one hell of a vehicle, designed with military use in mind, and had every advantage over other all-terrain trucks. Even so it was struggling to breach some of the mud formations and the increasing threat from the unrelenting rain.

The extreme weather conditions slowed his progress. He didn't sight the river until well into the afternoon. The heavy cloud formations laid a twilight shadow over the landscape. Bolan had noticed the increase in the dense growth of bush. There were more trees as well. He emerged from a wide spread of bush and saw the river ahead and to his right. Bolan pulled the Hummer into a grove of trees that were bending under the force from the downpour and cut the motor.

He studied the river from his position, watching the torrents of brown, muddy water foaming past. The volume of water was higher than it would have been normally. He saw debris being dragged along by the fierce current. An entire tree, twisting and rolling, was swept by. The soldier was thankful that he didn't have to reach the opposite bank. All he had to do was follow the river's course until it reached the sea.

Bolan took a brief rest period. He drank some water and ate some dry biscuits he had found in the knapsack. Leaning back in the seat, he stared through the windshield, rainwater streaming down the screen and distorting the images in front of him. Ahead he could see the swirling brown of the river, the dark trunks of trees and the green of foliage. He saw the merging of colors, rippling as he viewed them through the falling rain.

Bolan sat upright, his gaze fixed on the spot where he had seen a white flash.

It came again. A fleeting blur of white moving through the greenery ahead. Bolan took his Uzi and unlatched the Hummer's door. He stepped out, ignoring the downpour as he slipped into the deep cover of the trees and edged forward, keeping the spot in his field of vision. He kept moving for the next couple of minutes, reaching the edge of the trees. Crouching at the base of one thick trunk Bolan fixed his gaze on the distant spot and waited. His patience was rewarded minutes later when he saw the white shape again.

This time he identified it as a human figure, clad in white robes that covered it from head to foot. There was also some kind of white headdress, and beneath the turban he could see a dark face. He was looking at a man dressed in Arabic robes, with a leather belt around his waist and an automatic rifle in his hands. The man was moving in such a way as to suggest he was on patrol. Sentry duty.

Guarding what?

Had Bolan fallen lucky and found his slave traders? The

thought crossed his mind that they were sheltering from the storm, waiting out the rain before they continued their journey to the coast. He kept watch on the man, waiting until he turned away and moved back into the tangle of trees and bush. Bolan was able to follow the hazy white outline of the man's robes.

Once the sentry had almost faded from view, Bolan broke cover and sprinted across the open patch of ground until he was able to slip into the bush near where he had first seen the robed figure. The noise of the falling rain was intensified under the cover of the foliage and intertwining branches. The soft earth underfoot, comprising thick layers of leaf mold, had been turned spongy by the accumulating water. Bolan found himself ankle-deep in pools as he worked his way in the direction the white-robed figure had taken.

The roar of the flooded river was on Bolan's right. He occasionally glimpsed the brown rush of water through the trees.

Bolan spotted the white robe again. No more than twenty feet ahead. He drew back into shadow and kept the figure in sight. The man was still moving, but now he seemed to be out of his watcher's mode. Bolan crept forward, low to the ground, and closed the gap until he had only thick brush between him and his quarry.

The figure was standing still now. His rifle was slung by its strap from his left shoulder. His hands were gesticulating as he conversed with someone. It was only because of the downpour that Bolan couldn't hear him. Peering around the edge of the bush, Bolan saw that his initial guess had been correct to a degree.

There were four white-robed figures, all armed, standing over a huddled group of chained captives who squatted in the open, their eyes cowed, downcast. Bolan checked the captives over and saw they were all female. They appeared to range from as young as nine, ten years old to the late teens. He counted at least ten of them. The information he had gleaned from the rebel had the count as high as forty plus. He realized that this was only part of the slave traders' contingent, selected for a separate destination. He looked the captives over again.

And spotted Katherine Karima.

She stood out because of her modern, Western clothing. The others were all clad in robes or well-worn garments. Katherine's clothing was torn and stained, but identified her clearly. The Nike trainers she was wearing would have pointed her out if nothing else did.

Bolan didn't have to think too hard to come up with a sound reason why these young women had been singled out. The thought chilled him when he considered their likely destinations. The robed watchers of these females were trading in human lives, selling these unwilling young women for nothing more than cold, hard cash. The group was treated simply as merchandise. They had no choice in the matter. They were a commodity, taken at will and then sold off as living meat.

There was a moment when Bolan recalled the staring eyes of the dead boy he had buried. His fate had been sealed the second the slavers had snatched him from his home. His death would have meant nothing more than a loss of income to these dealers in human misery. With his selling value gone they had simply discarded him in the bush.

It was time to correct that action.

Bolan checked the Uzi. He was going to have to move fast. And there was only one way to do this. The way he saw it the slavers were waiting there to meet someone. This group was bound for a different destination from the rest of the captives. They must have stayed behind to join up with their buyer, Bolan thought, letting the main party carry on to the coast. The bad weather could have delayed the buyer, which might benefit Bolan if he initiated his move now.

But they might show up at any moment.

He couldn't wait any longer.

The Executioner placed his targets, stepped into view and shot the closest of the armed guards where he stood, the Uzi crackling with destructive power. As the white-robed figure twisted and fell, blood staining the front of his clothing, Bolan turned, bringing the Uzi on-line with his next target.

The sound of the submachine gun's stuttering burst galvanized the other guards into motion. For brief seconds they struggled to pinpoint the attacker, and Bolan used those seconds to his advantage. He swept the 9 mm SMG back and forth between the pair of guards standing within a couple of feet of each other. They stumbled back, kicked off balance by the tearing impact of the Uzi's slugs. Bolan fired a second time, raising the muzzle so his burst struck the targets in the head. They were driven to the ground in final moments of pain and confusion, their dying bodies shuddering from the deep wounds caused by the bullets from the Executioner's weapon.

The sound of a shot demanded Bolan's attention. He heard the shot splinter the trunk of a tree a few feet from his left side. The Executioner dropped to one knee, swinging the Uzi in a tight, controlled arc that came to a stop the moment he had the surviving slaver in his sights. Both men fired in the same fragment of time.

Bolan felt the slaver's bullet clip his sleeve, then his Uzi burst chewed into the man's face, turning it into a twisted, bloody mask. Two of the 9 mm rounds cored through to explode out the back of the slaver's skull. He uttered a single, startled cry as he toppled over and hit the wet ground heavily, body jerking in ugly spasms.

Turning, Bolan faced the huddled group. They had remained where they were, eyes lifted to stare at him in silence. Someone asked in perfect English, "Have you come to take us home?"

"Yes, Katherine Karima," Bolan said.

"Who are you?"

"My name is Mike Belasko. I'm helping your father."

Karima's daughter stood, regarding him with the look that only a ten-year-old could muster. "You look a mess."

"It's been a hard few days," Bolan told her.

He crossed to the dead slavers and went through their clothing until he located the keys that would unlock the shackles. He took a couple of the compact transceivers the slavers carried, pushing them into his blacksuit pockets. Returning to the captives he moved from one to another, unlocking the shackles they wore. He felt for each of the girls as the shackles fell away, exposing the raw, bloody marks the coarse iron had inflicted. Not one of them made any sound, bearing their pain with a dignity that surprised Bolan.

"Katherine, can you talk to them?" Bolan asked.

The girl nodded.

"Tell them they are free. Tell them the slave traders will not touch them again."

Katherine translated his words as she spoke to the others. One of them waited until she had finished then asked a question in return.

"She asks what should they do? They are a long way from home. They have no food. What will happen to them?"

It was a fair question. Bolan wasn't too sure what answer he was expected to give. He was going to have to play this one as it traveled.

"Katherine, I have to find these slavers. To get your brother back. Is he with the other group?"

The girl nodded. "They went that way," she said. "Following the river."

"Tell the others to follow me. I have transport back there."

The freed girls, almost as if on a silent command, clustered around Bolan, reaching out to touch his clothing. He looked into their faces, seeing at least a glimmer of hope returning to their previously hollow eyes. Now they began to speak, clamoring for attention. Some cried, releasing the feelings they had been forced to bottle up while they had been with the slavers.

"They are thanking you for giving them back their lives," Katherine explained, smiling as she translated the excited chatter. "They say you must be someone very special. Are you special, Mr. Belasko?"

"No. I'm just here to help."

Bolan led the way back to where he had left the Hummer. The girls followed him.

"Tell them to climb inside. It's going to be a tight fit but we don't have any choice."

One by one the girls climbed inside the Hummer, cramming themselves into the small space at the rear. Even though they were struggling for room, not one of them raised any protest. Bolan started the machine and moved off. As he drove he was attempting to come up with a solution regarding his charges. There was no way he could risk taking them too close with his upcoming contact with the rest of the slavers. Somewhere along this route he was going to have to find a place to hide them. Which was not the same as doing it in New York or Chicago. Here there were no safehouses. No local police. Bolan was on his own, not sure who was a friend and who was an enemy.

"Katherine, before the slave traders attacked and took you away, did you hear the rebels talking? Were you able to listen?"

"They didn't say a great deal. Mr. Belasko. They were not very nice people."

"I understand."

"When the slave traders attacked, I heard one of the rebels say something about Colonel Chakra."

Bolan glanced at her. "Do you remember?"

The girl nodded. "He said Colonel Chakra wouldn't be happy if we were taken by the slave traders. Losing his bargaining chips would hurt him badly. What is a bargaining chip, Mr. Belasko?"

"Something Colonel Chakra might soon choke on, Katherine."

"Oh," the girl said, not understanding.

"Katherine, one other thing. I don't want to upset you but..."

"Is it about Chembi?"

"The boy I found on the way in?"

Katherine nodded. She looked at Bolan with tears in her eyes. "It was so terrible. He wasn't strong. He found it hard to keep up but those men wouldn't listen. When he kept falling down they whipped him. Then one time he fell down and didn't get up even when they shouted at him and hit him. Mr. Belasko, why are people so cruel?"

Bolan had no answer to that question. All he could do was

reach out and put an arm around Katherine's slim shoulders, holding her as she wept.

The downpour stayed with them. It made the going slow, possibly harder due to the extra weight the Hummer was carrying. Bolan drove steadily, aware of his responsibility to his passengers, and also his commitment to returning Joseph Karima's children safely home to their father. It wasn't something Bolan carried lightly. Nor did he allow it to deter him from the path he had chosen.

An hour after they had set off Katherine Karima tugged at Bolan's sleeve. "There's a man out there," she said, and her matter-of-fact tone warned him she wasn't fantasizing.

Bolan eased the Hummer to a stop, peering through the side window in the direction the girl was indicating. Initially he thought he was seeing things, then the tall figure moved, emerging from the mist and placing himself directly in front of the vehicle. There was something familiar about the man. Bolan climbed out of the Hummer, his Uzi held loosely at his side. He used his sleeve to wipe the rain from his eyes. After taking a closer look he relaxed.

The tall figure of Jomo's Tempai friend, Ashansii, moved to meet him. The African raised his hand in greeting.

"Belasko."

"Ashansii."

The rain glistened on Ashansii's black features as he looked over Bolan's shoulder at the Hummer and the anxious faces pressed to the windows. He frowned, not understanding.

"Wait," Bolan said, holding up both hands. He glanced over his shoulder. "Katherine. I need you."

She came running from the Hummer to stand at Bolan's side, staring up at the tall Ashansii.

"Can you talk with him? Understand him, I mean?"

Katherine spoke to Ashansii. He nodded and replied to her question.

"Yes," she said. "What do you want me to ask him?"

"How did he get here?"

Ashansii listened to Katherine, then raised an arm and gesticulated excitedly.

"His people were moving their cattle toward the river. Looking for a place to rest them where there was water because the hot weather has dried up water holes."

"Tell him that our good friend and warrior, Jomo, is dead. He was killed by the rebels."

Katherine translated. The expression on Ashansii's face was genuine. He looked at Bolan and spoke.

"He says Jomo was a true Tempai. He asks if you need help."

Through Katherine, Bolan explained his situation and his need to have the girls moved somewhere safe. Ashansii offered the sanctuary of his band. They would take the girls to a place he knew. Somewhere that only the nomadic Tempai had knowledge of.

"They will be safe with me," Ashansii said. "Are you going to avenge Jomo?"

"Yes. And bring this girl's brother to safety."

Bolan returned to the Hummer and picked up Jomo's carbine. He also brought some extra magazines. "Do you know how to use this weapon?"

Ashansii nodded. "Just because I carry a spear does not mean I am not familiar with these guns."

Bolan handed over the weapon. "Jomo would have been happy to know his gun is in the hands of his friend."

Ashansii hesitated before he asked, "Did he die a warrior's death?"

"His enemies fell before him. Ashansii, I owe my life to Jomo."

"When you have killed Jomo's enemies, come back to this place and I will look out for you. Now bring the children."

Bolan took out one of the transceivers he had taken from the dead slavers. He showed it to Katherine. "I'm sure you know how to use this," he said.

She looked the transceiver over, nodding.

Bolan set the frequency to match the one he was keeping.

"When I can I'll contact you to let you know everything is okay. We can use these to find each other. Don't use it until tomorrow. Only turn it on for a short time or you'll drain the power pack. Bring the girls now."

When Ashansii saw the marks of the shackles on the girls' wrists he asked, "They were taken by slave traders?"

"Yes. There are others being taken to the coast. They will be placed on a ship and taken away."

Ashansii spat on the ground. "Kill them. Let them see we don't want them in our country."

Katherine looked up at Bolan.

"Can't I come with you, Mr. Belasko?"

"I need to move fast to catch them. They won't stand by when I try to bring the captives and your brother back. It's not a place you need to be. Go with Ashansii. His people will look after you until this is over."

Bolan watched the group vanish in the gloom. He returned to the Hummer and moved off. With the girls gone he was able to concentrate fully on what lay ahead. There were no distractions. Nothing to draw his attention from the job at hand.

YUSEF AND HANNI TOOK their time inspecting the dead slavers. They picked up the tracks Bolan and the girls had left on their way to the parked Hummer.

"An hour," Yusef said.

"More," Hanni disagreed. "Two hours."

Yusef activated the transceiver and contacted Sergeant Masson.

"The American found some of the slavers. They had stopped with a number of the captives. Waiting for someone perhaps. Belasko killed the four slavers and took the captives away in the Hummer. Maybe two hours ago."

"Keep after him. He may have Karima's children with him now. If you locate him don't do anything that might put the children in danger. We need them alive."

"We understand."

Yusef switched off the transceiver and clipped it to his belt. He tapped Hanni on the shoulder. "Let's go."

15

Simon Chakra twisted in his copilot's seat and spoke to the radio operator of the SA-330 Puma helicopter, ordering him to make contact with Sergeant Masson and inform him they were on their way. Masson's earlier contact, alerting Chakra that Belasko had already clashed with some of the slave traders and the signs were that he had freed a number of the captives, hadn't gone down well. Chakra's response, though expected, had been unsettling. Masson was left in no doubt that the military commander held him personally responsible.

The base helicopter had returned by this time. Chakra had ordered it refueled immediately. He had assembled his pilot and radio operator and the Puma had been back in the air within the hour.

His mind was alive with a multitude of thoughts. He knew he needed to calm down and not allow himself to become too wrapped up in the negative side of the problem. He needed to revise his plans, to deal with the current situation, resolve it and then bring everything back on track. Control was the watchword. He had to take control.

Hector Campos was seated at the rear of the Puma, calmly watching events unfold. The Cuban had the ability to draw

himself away from whatever confusion was created and ana-
lyze the situation carefully before he made a decision. When
he did make his choice nothing seemed to be left to chance.
Simon Chakra admitted his main fault was his lack of control sometimes. It was handy when it came to bawling out one
of his men for making a mistake, but it hardly served himself
when he had his own problems and felt he was losing command. Until his resolve to initiate the rebellion against Joseph
Karima, Chakra's main problems had been those involved in
combat and logistics. He had a fine chain of command under
him and it was easy to pass along responsibility to his subor-
dinates. Times were different now. His covert activities included consorting with the main rebel force, negotiating help
from the Cubans and dealing with the myriad matters that
came out of all that.

The Cubans had been only too pleased to help. Africa was
one of their main concerns, and fomenting unrest was something they reveled in. Hector Campos had been a strong ally
the moment he became Chakra's advisor. There had been the
secret trips to Cuba, then the cash that had been offered to
Chakra as a sweetener, ensuring that even if the rebellion
didn't go as well as planned, he would always have something
to fall back on. He accepted the money, well aware that it was
there to buy his loyalty; he had to smile when he thought about
the cash, safe in his deposit account in the Cayman Islands.
The Cubans might still be strong on the Marxist philosophy,
but they had no embarrassment when it came to handing over
what was nothing more than a good old-fashioned bribe. Cuba
would have been quick to take account of the vast copper deposits Tempala held. Something they wouldn't be averse to
having a share of if Chakra's coup succeeded.

Behind Chakra the radio operator said, "Colonel, sir, I have Sergeant Masson for you."

Chakra took the microphone that was handed to him. He indicated to the operator that he wanted the exchange to be played over the speaker.

"Well, Sergeant? I hope this is better news than last time."

"I had a call from the trackers about twenty minutes ago, Colonel. They're finding it difficult to follow Belasko's tracks because of the storm. Too much water. It's simply washing away tracks before anyone can spot them."

"Is that the best excuse you can come up with, Sergeant?"

"With respect, Colonel, it is not an excuse. This rain is coming down so hard it's almost impossible to see more than twenty feet."

"Have you forgotten, Sergeant, that I am flying through the storm myself? Don't use the weather as a way of concealing your incompetence."

"Listen to me, Colonel, you may well be my commanding officer, and I will follow you to the last man, but do not accuse me of incompetence. Court martial me if you want. Right now I don't give a damn because I'm nearly up to my armpits in water and we can't track Belasko in this weather."

"I won't be spoken to this way, Masson."

"Then get yourself down on the ground, Colonel, and show me how to find Belasko in this storm. If you do I'll charge myself with insubordination. If not then the hell with it."

There was a click as Masson ended the transmission, leaving Chakra staring out through the rain-lashed screen of the helicopter, keeping his mouth closed because he had no idea what to say. There was a hush within the cabin. No one spoke for a while. Chakra handed the headset back to the radio operator, then turned to the front again. The operator quietly clicked off the speaker in case there were any more heated exchanges.

Chakra heard someone moving, then sensed someone standing behind his seat. He caught a whiff of the spicy aftershave Campos wore.

"He's probably right, Simon," Campos said quietly. "Take a look at that rain. Give the man his due. And if he dares speak to you the way he did I'd say he's too good to lock up."

Chakra cleared his throat. "The truth is, Hector, you're right. But I'll make him smart for talking to me like that in front of my men."

"He probably didn't realize you had the speaker on. Masson was talking to you man to man."

"My God, Hector, you should become a politician."

"Let's face it, Simon, Castro can't live forever."

"Colonel," the pilot interrupted. "It's going to be dark in an hour. If this weather holds we could have problems if we don't land soon."

"Find a good spot and take us down. We can sleep in here and start out again at dawn. Belasko will be under the same conditions so he won't be going too far tonight."

THE STORM WAS SHOWING no signs of abating. The rain was sweeping in from the coast, a strong wind bringing the full power of the downpour. Twice Bolan had struggled to keep the Hummer moving. He realized he was putting himself at risk if he tried to keep going in these conditions. The same would apply to whoever might be on his trail. It looked as if the severe weather would curtail all movement through the night. The slave traders, despite their direct line for the coast, would have to make a temporary camp for the night and start off again at first light. Bolan hoped the storm would blow itself out by dawn.

He found a place where he could park just inside a wide spread of bush. The section he chose was on a rise, which would keep him comparatively safe from flooding. Bolan backed the vehicle into the bush and cut the motor. The thick growth reached almost level with the Hummer's low roofline.

Bolan checked all his weapons before he settled down, the Uzi across his lap, and scanned the rain-washed terrain around him. From where he was he could see the sheets of rain bowling in across the landscape. The raw power of the rain, sluicing down out of the lowering gray sky, came crashing down on the land. He saw brush bending under the weight of the water. Trees were curving, their branches sagging until, in some cases, they snapped off under the pressure.

He dozed fitfully, his senses still active, ready to snap him back to full alert at any sign of danger. It was a way of recharging his batteries without letting himself become open to attack. The threat from the opposition was bound to come sooner or later. Bolan had no illusions on that score. Staying ahead of them wouldn't last forever. The odds were against his being able to avoid them indefinitely. When it did happen he wanted to be ready, and part of being ready was the ability to be at full strength both mentally and physically.

The rain maintained its presence through the long hours, only starting to ease off in the pre-dawn. The downpour continued, but it lost a degree of intensity.

In the half light Bolan found himself looking at the radio transmitter built into the Hummer. He hadn't done anything with the set since driving away from the base. Wary of having any communications picked up by the opposition, Bolan had voted to leave the radio switched off. His time had been occupied with making contact with the slave traders, so the radio hadn't been uppermost in his mind. Now, with time slipping away and pursuit close behind, Bolan debated whether to risk giving away his location by making a transmission.

Bolan reached out and powered up the radio. He set it to receive only and worked his way through the dial, listening to the mix of voices coming through. He couldn't risk contacting anyone in Tempala. The situation was too fragile for that. No matter whom he got through to, Bolan had no guarantees if the person was genuine or if he might be working for the Chakra/terrorist alliance. He needed to contact a party isolated from Tempala and its covert operations.

Bolan sat upright as he heard an American accent. He listened for a while to convince himself he was hearing correctly. Picking up the handset Bolan locked in the setting and flipped the switch to transmit.

AARON KURTZMAN acknowledged the incoming message and saved it. He picked up the telephone and put a call through to Hal Brognola.

"Hal, you'd better get over here pretty quickly. We just received a message from Striker, via the U.S. Navy. He needs some backup and you need to call the President."

"This needs to be one to one, sir," Brognola explained to the Man when he called a few minutes later. "The situation in Tempala is on the edge. We don't know who we can trust. You can get directly through to Joseph Karima. Pass along the information Striker has given us. At least it gives Karima a chance to pick his people and decide what to do."

"I'll do it now," the President said. "When can you get here?"

"I'm leaving immediately, sir. And bringing all the data with me," he stated before hanging up. Turning to Barbara Price "Give Jack a call," he said. "Have him fire up a chopper. We're leaving for Washington."

JOSEPH KARIMA STARED at the rain sluicing down the window of his office. He was experiencing a strange mix of emotions. The main one concerned the news about his daughter. He found he couldn't decide whether to be overjoyed at the rescue of one of his children or worried that he still didn't have both of them back.

The revelation that Simon Chakra was one of the key players in the rebel movement, and had also been party to the kidnapping of his children, had shocked Karima. In his own words he hadn't known whom to trust. Now reality was proving how correct he had been. Even so the revelation hurt. Over the years he had maintained his confidence in Chakra. Outwardly the man had done a superb job, bringing Tempala's small military presence up to the mark. How long had he been working behind the scenes building his own force of loyal supporters alongside the rebel faction?

Karima didn't dwell on the past mistakes. He needed to be strong now, the leader his people looked to. It was time for him to take control and assert himself. It might be bloody, and there was no guarantee he would survive. Whatever the outcome, Joseph Karima would not be found wanting.

Leaning forward he picked up his cell phone and called one of the speed-dial numbers. It was answered instantly.

"Raymond, I'm in my office. Can you get over here straight away? Thank you."

When Nkoya arrived twenty minutes later, wet from running through the rain from his car, Karima was ready for him.

"Joseph? What is it?" the vice-president asked.

Karima embraced his old friend. "First I owe you an apology."

"For what?"

"Please, let me explain. First about Mike Belasko. He has nothing to do with Ambassador Leland Cartwright. Belasko was sent by the President of the U.S.A. to look into the kidnapping of Katherine and Randolph. This was after I had called on the President for help."

Nkoya nodded gently. "Because you had no one to turn to in your own administration," he said, "you couldn't know who was a friend or who was the enemy. Any of us could be in league with the rebels. I understand. Go on."

Karima stared at his vice-president. He was lost for words.

"Joseph, I understand," Nkoya repeated.

"But I put you among those I was unsure of. To my shame, Raymond, I couldn't even tell you why Belasko was here."

"In your position I would have done exactly the same. Your children had been taken."

"How long have we been friends? Years, Raymond, yet I shut you out. I realize now it was a terrible thing to do. I can only offer you my sincere regret."

Nkoya smiled. "Joseph, what are friends for? Now why have you sent for me at this ungodly hour?"

"Belasko has found Katherine. He has her back. Now he is going after the men who have Randolph."

"Where do the rebels have him?"

"Not rebels, Raymond. It appears that the men who took the children were attacked by slave traders. The slavers took the children. Belasko found this out during a clash with part of a covert military group in league with the rebels."

It was Nkoya's turn to look surprised. "Military?"

"Belasko has proof that Simon Chakra is our traitor. He has his own agenda. He's in with the rebels."

Nkoya settled into a moment of deep thought.

"Then we will have to step carefully, Joseph. If Chakra has his own people involved we'll need to assemble a force to combat him." He paused, looking at Karima and smiling suddenly. "Now I can understand how you felt."

"Belasko managed to get a message to his people in America via a link with the U.S. Navy. He has a location where the slave traders are to meet a ship on the coast. I have the coordinates. But Belasko has people hunting for him. I just wish we were in a position to help him."

MACK BOLAN HAD CHANGED location after his radio transmission. He took the Hummer farther west, finding travel a little easier now the storm showed signs of abating. He maintained his travel until he found himself on a high bluff overlooking the confluence of river and ocean. There the river widened dramatically. The hard flow caused by the storm was slowed by the expansion of the estuary, though the water was still fast moving, flowing strongly. Beyond the tip of the land the Atlantic clashed with the river and Bolan could see the foaming mass of water even in the gloom of the early dawn.

He had decided to leave the vehicle. If his transmission had been intercepted and a location plotted, the Hummer would be the initial target of those following him. Bolan suited up and put the knapsack on his back, into which he had placed as much spare ammunition for his weapons as possible, as well as a good supply of the grenades he'd located. The Uzi went across his chest, loaded and ready for use, hanging by its sling. He took one of the SA-80 carbines, fully loaded with a double magazine. That would be his primary weapon until he exhausted the ammo supply, then he would turn to the Uzi. He carried an extra magazine for the carbine in the pockets of his blacksuit.

As he exited the Hummer Bolan felt the beat of the falling rain. There was a wind blowing in from the ocean, pushing the rain into his face. He raised the hood of the Hummer and used his knife to sever a number of connections, disabling the vehicle. He was denying himself use of the vehicle, but it was worth it if it also meant the opposition couldn't use it either.

Bolan lowered his head, chin almost on his chest as he set the pace for his slog across the waterlogged ground. His boots sank deep into the spongy surface and he was forced to adopt a steady, deliberate rhythm to keep from becoming bogged down.

YUSEF AND HANNI found the abandoned Hummer a short time after Bolan had moved off. It was light by this time. The trackers examined the damage Bolan had inflicted on the vehicle before Yusef clicked on his transceiver and spoke to Masson.

"I believe he is not far ahead," Yusef said. "We will carry on and catch him soon."

Hanni had moved forward, checking the ground. He began to wave his arm. Cutting the transmission, Yusef rejoined his partner.

"Here," Hanni said. He was down on one knee, indicating faint marks in the soft earth. "See. Boot prints."

Yusef saw the faint outlines. The rain water had already

submerged them but the depressed grass and earth had still not faded. The print was there to be seen by such a trained eye as Hanni. He stood and ran forward a number of yards before pausing again.

"Still west," Hanni said. "That way. Toward the coast. Four, maybe fives miles. Can you smell the sea?"

Yusef stood beside his partner. He could detect the salty tang in the air himself.

"We've got him," he said. "Time for Belasko to die."

16

By nine-thirty the rain had stopped completely. The sea breeze pushed the clouds inland and the sun broke through shortly after. Within an hour it was starting to get hot again, pale wreaths of steam rising from the wet earth. Africa's weather cycle remained as it had for centuries. The thirsty earth swallowed the rain and the vegetation took on a new, vibrant appearance. The greenery gleamed with life and flowering plants blossomed in abundance.

As far as Bolan was concerned the weather change made little difference. Conflict, death and the treachery of man remained constant. He had already chosen his path, committed himself to whatever confronted him at its end, and rain or shine, it would come.

He crouched in a dense forested area, scanning the curving strip of white sand that spread out before him. The beach was deserted. According to the map he was still carrying, and studying even as he checked out his surroundings, the location of the village Kurtzman had given him lay a few miles in a southerly direction. Bolan folded the map and stuffed it back in his pocket. He picked up his autorifle and prepared to move off.

Bolan froze, making no great show of having heard sound behind him.

He slipped his finger through the SA-80's trigger guard. His senses, tuned to pick up any extraneous sound while Bolan had been concentrating on something else, hadn't let him down. Bolan listened again and located the source. Behind and to his left. He recalled a deep growth of foliage back there. Dense enough to conceal a man, but grown so close that it would be difficult to negotiate without disturbing the vegetation.

He allowed himself a fleeting question on the identity of the intruder.

One of the slavers? A tail-ender keeping an eye on the back trail?

Or one of the people following him? Rebel, terrorist, covert military? As far as Bolan was concerned they were all from the same mold.

He didn't care who. They had marked themselves by their own actions, laying themselves open to the Executioner's brand of settlement.

The soft click of a safety being freed made Bolan smile. Leaving that a little too late did nothing more than advertise the intruder's presence. More soft rustling of the foliage finally gave Bolan the target acquisition he needed, and he came up on one knee, the SA-80 rising with him, turning at the waist.

Bolan saw a lean figure half-risen from his place of concealment, leaning forward for a clear shot. The man had a weapon similar to the one the Executioner was tracking him with. Bolan's finger stroked the SA-80's trigger. He felt the recoil nudge his shoulder. Then he fired twice and saw his shots strike, impacting with the intruder chest high. The 5.56 mm slugs punched deep holes in the lean torso, knocking the target back, arms flying wide apart. Red blossomed across the man's clothing. The stricken man stumbled awkwardly, already losing his coordination, pain swiftly replacing the initial numbness. He staggered forward, going almost to his knees, his weapon falling from his hands. He threw out one arm, trying to brace himself, and caught Bolan's follow-up burst in the upper chest and throat. Gagging against the blood rising in his throat he began to cough, bloody strings of fluid erupting from his lips as he fell facedown on the ground.

YUSEF SAW HANNI GO DOWN, his disbelief turning swiftly to anger. Until this moment he had never allowed sentiment to cloud his judgement. But this was different. He and Hanni had been a team for too many years. They had lived and fought together to the point where they seldom had to ask what the other was thinking or going to do. Through lean times, hard times, and many good times, Yusef and Hanni had been the best trackers in Tempala.

Now all that was gone, brushed aside in an instant because just for once Hanni had allowed his overeager nature to make him careless. Instead of waiting a little longer, Hanni had decided to act first, believing he had the man named Belasko in his sights, ready for the kill. Yusef had been moments away from settling into his own position, from where he and Hanni would have had Belasko in a crossfire.

But Hanni had jumped in too quickly, moved without due care and had alerted Belasko. The result of that error lay facedown on the forest floor, his blood spread around him.

The moment passed by, bringing Yusef to the present, and the man called Belasko only a few feet in front of him. Yusef slipped the keen-edged panga from its waist sheath and drew his right arm across his chest, ready to strike the blow that would end it all.

BOLAN WAS PULLING BACK from his encounter with the African, having seen him hit the ground, and from his rear he heard the muted rustle of clothing against foliage. He stayed low, turning, bringing the SA-80 up in a defensive gesture.

He saw the blur of the African's shape as the man made his play. The blade of the panga was already on the downswing. With nothing else to protect him Bolan pushed his autorifle forward.

The blade of the panga struck with a solid whack, the impact jarring against Bolan's hands. The Executioner recovered and swung the SA-80, clubbing the man across the lower jaw. The soldier dropped the rifle and reached out to grasp handfuls of the rebel's loose clothing. Using the man's forward motion, Bolan half rose, turning so that he could throw the African over his hip. At the same time Bolan used both hands to haul him forward, the man's own bulk and momentum doing the rest. The rebel was thrown over Bolan's hip, his feet leaving the ground. His overturned body slammed into the trunk of a tree. The man gagged as the breath was hammered from his lungs. He hit the sodden earth with a hard thump. The panga slipped from fingers on impact. The rebel gathered himself and rolled, turning over, and scrambled to get his feet under him. He searched for the panga.

Bolan rammed into the African chest high, slamming his shoulder into the rebel's torso. Locked together, the two men went down with a hard crash, Bolan on top, already reaching for the man's throat, twisting and dragging the rebel closer to him. The rebel reached up to clutch at the powerful forearm that had snapped tight against his throat. He struggled frantically, kicking out in vain, his breath already shutting off. Bolan placed his free hand against the back of the rebel's head and shoved down hard, pushing the man's face into the waterlogged earth. The African's desperate attempt to draw air in only brought him a mouthful of water as Bolan pressed his face harder into the spongy forest carpet. He choked, coughing and trying to spit out the water, but the pressure on the back of his head was unrelenting. The man panicked, thrashing wildly, doing little except speed his demise. He might have tried to scream but he was incapable of making any sound now. His struggles began to subside as more fluid was sucked into his starved lungs.

And then he relaxed, all resistance gone.

Bolan released the dead man's body and pushed himself to his knees. He reached for the SA-80 carbine. The rebel's panga had scored the metal barrel. The rifle had saved Bolan's life. Standing upright, Bolan checked the area, the carbine's muzzle probing the shadows. He saw nothing, heard nothing. By the look of the clothing the two men had worn, he decided they must be part of the group following him. Possibly scouts for the main party. That meant the others wouldn't be far behind.

Bolan moved off, picking up his pace as he pushed through the trees and foliage, his destination, as before, the deserted village on the beach.

17

Simon Chakra turned away from examining the bodies, shaking his head in quiet disgust at the inadequacy of the people under his command. He walked by Sergeant Masson without a word, glancing to where Hector Campos stood apart from the rest of the group. Campos caught his eye, giving a slight shrug.

"One he shoots, the other he drowns in rainwater," Chakra said wearily. "Who is this man?"

"The kind you could do with on your side?" Campos said lightly, unable to resist the temptation.

Chakra chose to ignore the jibe. He raised himself to his full height, staring up through the trees at the wide blue sky. He pulled off his fatigue hat and ran a hand through his hair. This wasn't the way it was supposed to go. Planning and preparation were flying out the window. The American was making a mockery of everything. He appeared to have some kind of good-luck charm accompanying him that allowed him to walk through fire and over water. If not, he had some kind of death wish that blanked out all thought of personal risk. If Chakra had believed in magic, as some of the tribal elders did, he might have seen Belasko as a spirit warrior, one who couldn't be harmed by mortal enemies.

Sergeant Masson approached cautiously, eager to carry on but not wanting to find himself on the receiving end of Chakra's anger.

"Colonel? The men are ready to move out."

"Then do it, Sergeant, and for God's sake catch him this time."

"Sir," Masson said, saluting.

Chakra waved him aside. "Just remember to keep me informed." He crossed over to Campos. "Time we were in the air as well. I won't let this mercenary of Karima's play with us. I'll kill the bastard myself and hang his head on a hook outside Government House."

He made his way toward the Puma, which sat out in the open, beyond the forest area. As soon as he was in sight of the aircraft, Chakra raised his arm to the pilot, circling his finger. The rotors began to turn, the pilot powering up the twin turbines in readiness for takeoff.

AS FAR AS SERGEANT MASSON was concerned, the old adage that professionals never took anything personally was just a load of bullshit. Yusef and Hanni had been his trackers for a long time. He wasn't about to forget that in a hurry, and the hell with Chakra's devotion to duty. Masson was going to catch Belasko. He was going to see to it that the man died. And unless Masson was in chains, or dead, nothing was going to deter him from that.

He dispersed his squad. They were going in on foot from here. No point in clanking around in the Land Rover, which wasn't the most silent of vehicles. They had the slave traders to consider as well as Belasko, and it wouldn't be wise to advertise their approach by doing so in a chugging Land Rover.

The American was somewhere ahead of them, making his

way along the edge of the beach. He had the knowledge about the slavers' whereabouts. Masson wanted to use that knowledge to guide him and his squad in. Once contact was made, the slave traders and Belasko would be Masson's objective.

Since the storm had blown over, the temperature had risen with a vengeance. Moving through the forested area was akin to being inside a steam bath. The trapped heat and moisture created a close, humid atmosphere, and before long Masson and his squad were all sweating, their uniforms soaked and clinging to their flesh. The scarf Masson wore around his neck, loose and long so he could use it to wipe his face, was soaked within the first half hour.

Underfoot the forest floor was soft and oozed water with every step. Insects flitted back and forth, some of them seeming to have a fetish for human flesh. They alighted on a regular basis and no amount of swatting them away proved very successful.

"Sergeant," one of the soldiers called.

He was the squad radio operator and carried a com unit on his back. As Masson joined him the soldier held out a handset. Masson put it to his ear.

"Chakra here, Masson. Anything to report?"

"No contact yet, Colonel. Belasko has almost two hours on us. I have the men spread so we can cover a wider area. Once we make contact I'll call."

"Very well, Sergeant. We will stay well to the rear until we hear from you. Can't afford to warn Belasko, or the slave traders, we're around."

Masson passed the handset to the radio operator. "Try and keep him out of my hair, Jando. At least until we find that American."

CHAKRA HAD ONLY JUST SETTLED back after his call to Masson when he was informed of an incoming call by his radio operator. He had the call switched through to his headset.

"Chakra speaking."

"Colonel, this is Zimbala."

"Go ahead."

"We have been making assessments in the city. Checking our people. Testing the mood."

"And?"

"We can't be sure but the atmosphere is very odd. It's as if everyone is waiting for something to happen."

"Not surprising with what's going on in the country."

"No. The city is unusually quiet," Zimbala insisted.

"Not been setting any more bombs off then?"

"That is not funny, Colonel."

"Neither was blowing up half a city block to make a point we had already established."

"Karima needed reminding how serious we are."

"That point had been made by taking his children. The idea was to achieve our aim without resorting to methods liable to put even our own people against us."

"We've already reviewed that. We had lost his pups to the slave traders."

"But he didn't fucking well know that. Damn it, Rudolph, we could have played out the kidnapping ploy and still got what we wanted. But you and that lunatic Harruri couldn't wait. You had to go and make a grand gesture. Just as a matter of interest, have you conducted a survey of the families of the dead from the bomb blast? We must be at the top of their popularity poll at this moment in time."

"This is a war we are fighting. For our nation. For our identity. Have you forgotten that, Simon?"

"I don't need reminding what I'm fighting for, Rudolph. But we won't advance our cause by blowing up the damn city and turning the population into bloody martyrs. Keeping the faith with the Kirandi isn't going to be easy now you've killed some of them in the bomb explosion."

"Sacrifice is part of any struggle for freedom."

"Sacrifice for the cause should be a voluntary consideration, Rudolph. Outright slaughter is another matter."

Zimbala was silent for a moment. "Tell me, Colonel, how is your little campaign going? Have you cornered your American yet?"

"We are closing in on him as we speak. The matter will be resolved shortly."

"How soon?"

"Rudolph, this is a military exercise. It doesn't work to a timetable. Things change and we have to work within those parameters. The storm added to our difficulties but that is over now."

"I see. So how does this fit in with our previous agenda?"

"It means we have to adjust the time scale accordingly, Rudolph. Please don't play mind games with me. You understand the situation so stop implying you don't."

"Very well, Colonel. No more games."

RUDOLPH ZIMBALA ENDED the transmission. He replaced the handset and leaned back in his seat, peering across the room and catching the eye of Shempi Harruri.

"Is the savior Colonel having problems?" Harruri asked.

"That man is a liability. He's out there playing soldiers and chasing that American all over the country. We took Karima's children and lost them to the slavers. As far as I'm concerned we should let the slavers keep them. The more I think about it the better it sounds. Karima's kids being sold off to some hard labor sweatshop, making car batteries, or digging in some mine is what they deserve. Karima would never survive that."

Harruri crossed the room. He was a lean, hollow-cheeked man. A thin cigarette dangled from the corner of his mouth. He smoked constantly. He stood beside a stack of SA-80 carbines, part of the latest cache the rebels had taken delivery of, trailing a hand across the weapons.

"We should go ahead," he said. "I'm tired of waiting for Chakra and his fucking toy soldiers. We could take Government House in a few hours. Walk right up to Karima's office and blow his brains out. Who's going to stop us? This isn't about Chakra saving face. It's about stopping Karima from making his deals with the Americans. Signing away the rights to our copper and letting the American military set up a base at Rugendi Bay."

"You think we're ready for that, Shempi? It's a big step up from what we've been doing. Once we start there's no going back."

"You think I don't know that? This is what we've been working up to. Rudolph, we knew this day had to come. Why the hell have we been collecting all these weapons? Rifles. Grenades. Rocket launchers. We have our people in the city. Karima is so tied up with getting his kids back he won't be thinking about anything else. If we strike now we can take the city and the administration center. We take control and the country is ours. The Kirandi will be behind us once we show them we are in command. Now is the time, Rudolph. If we wait for Chakra we lose the moment."

Zimbala felt himself become enthused by his friend's words. He was torn between waiting and striking immediately, aware that either way had a risk factor. Life didn't follow the rule book. They could decide to keep waiting, searching for that perfect moment before they went ahead with their strike against Karima's power base.

What perfect moment?

How did they guarantee the day? The time?

He admitted they couldn't. Putting off their strike only allowed Karima time to strengthen his own position.

"Shempi, let's hope we don't live to regret this."

Harruri smiled, lighting a fresh cigarette. "If we don't get it right," he said, "we won't live long enough to regret it." He said it without a trace of emotion in his voice.

"Let's do it," Zimbala said.

AS THE CALLS WENT OUT across the city, the rebel cells moved quickly to prepare themselves. Hidden arms caches were unsealed and weapons passed out. Each cell had its own particular assignment and made its way to its appointed position. Watches had already been synchronized.

Midday was the time. At twelve o'clock the Kirandi rebels would step into the history books.

The village had been the center of a fishing settlement, now long abandoned. When it had been occupied the treeline had been cut back and the thick, lush foliage kept at bay. That had been reversed now. The forest was reclaiming its former ground, the vegetation starting to engulf the empty huts, invading the deserted interiors. Along the beach lay the rotting hulls of fishing boats. Nets and lobster pots were scattered about the area.

Mack Bolan's attention was occupied with current matters. Such as the chained and huddled group of around forty captives, overlooked by half a dozen armed slave traders. Bolan had made his situation assessment in the ten minutes he had been crouched in the thick foliage of the forested area adjacent to the beach.

Beyond the sand lay the blue-watered bay, waves rolling in to break against the white sand. The bay was about a quarter mile across at its entrance. Curving points of land swept around to encircle the inlet, protecting it from the heavier swell of the Atlantic beyond its confines.

The Executioner had another problem to add to his list.

The arrival of the slavers' pickup ship. The vessel had appeared a few minutes ago, steaming slowly into sight around the bay's northern promontory. There was nothing glamorous about the ship. It was a single-funnel rust bucket, the kind seen regularly in the coastal sea lanes. They were the equivalent of 18-wheel rigs that plied the highways, picking up cargo for delivery and loading up again for the return run. These ships were workhorses. No one paid them much attention, and this was why the slave traders had chosen such a vessel for their business. The difference was in the cargo this particular ship carried. Not stacks of timber or agricultural machinery. Whatever the paper manifests said, the cargo this steamer carried was human.

Bolan watched the ship move in across the bay, coming about two hundred yards off shore. He saw the anchor drop. A wooden gangway was swung out and down the side of the ship. Figures moved around on deck. A couple of motor boats were lowered into the water, heading toward the beach.

The armed guards on the beach began to rouse the captives, dividing them into groups of six. The first two groups were herded to the water's edge. The moment the boats hit the beach the captives were forced on board. Any who resisted were roughly handled. There was no hesitation in the action of the armed guards as they used rifle butts to load the captives into the motorboats. The first batch were taken across to the waiting ship and unceremoniously herded up the swaying gangway.

Watching and evaluating his options, Bolan decided his choices were limited. The captives were already being taken out to the ship, so any action he undertook had to include those on board. Which meant in simple terms that he had to get on the ship himself.

The first part of his plan required getting out to the ship.

With his decision made, Bolan set to solving the problem. He had already noticed that one of the armed guards was patrolling the dividing line between beach and treeline. The man had a line of travel that brought him up to and past Bolan's place of concealment. He had walked by a number of times, unaware how close he was to Bolan's position.

The slaver made yet another pass. At the point where he crossed Bolan's path the guard was at the farthest point from his companions, who were fully occupied supervising the loading of the captives.

There was no warning. The guard trod the same path he had for the past hour, moving in the regular, almost mechanical way that befalls any guard after a long period of doing the same thing over and over. He heard only a fleeting whisper of sound before a powerful arm snaked around his neck, drawing tight. A hand pressed against the back of his head, pushing it forward. With his air cut off, the guard started to panic. He dropped his rifle and reached up to try to free the arm encircling his neck, but he was already starting to choke. Bolan pulled him back into the trees, away from the beach. His body banged against the trunks of the palms fringing the edge of the beach as he kicked out in terror. His struggles only exhausted the limited air in his lungs and he fought a losing battle as Bolan hauled him off his feet, the whole of his weight suspended from the arm around his neck. He kicked out with no success. His life ebbed away swiftly, his resistance waning, and in the end his lifeless form hung limp and still in the Executioner's grip.

Lowering the guard to the ground, Bolan loosened the man's robe and stripped it from the body. He pulled it on over his own weapons, fastening the belt at the waist. He adjusted the turban headdress, then pulled the loose hood over his head. The flapping folds covered his face in shadow. Bolan let the long sleeves of the robe fall to cover his hands. He stepped out of the trees and retrieved the rifle the guard had dropped, then turned and mimicked the man's former patrol.

Bolan could see that the power boats were on the way out to the ship with yet another cargo. He maintained his patrolling, counting down the minutes to the last trip the boats would make. Then his deception would either convince the other slavers or he would be unmasked quickly. Bolan was prepared for either eventuality. If it came to making his play before he reached the ship, so be it.

The final groups of captives were herded into the boats. Bolan, covertly watching the activity, was ready when one of the guards turned in his direction and called to him. Bolan raised a hand in acknowledgment and made his way toward the waiting boats. The rest of the guards were already in the boats, leaving a space for Bolan at the stern of one. He splashed through the water, head down, and hauled himself over the stern, settling himself on the flat plank that served as a seat. The huddled group of captives was between Bolan and the other slavers in the boat. They were in the center, around the wheelman. The moment Bolan was on board the engine was powered up and the boat moved away from the beach, following in the wake of the first boat.

Bolan slipped his finger inside the trigger guard of the SA-80. He sat motionless, eyes and ears alert for any sign of discovery, but the other men were occupied with the captives. Leaning out to the side Bolan watched the bulk of the slave ship growing larger. As they got closer he could see the peeling paint and streaks of rust that stained the hull of the vessel. Water was pumping from the bilge outlets and Bolan could hear the dull thump of the idling diesel engines.

He felt the boat slow, the motor throttling back while the first boat unloaded its cargo. It seemed to take a long time and Bolan expected to be spoken to at any time. Again nothing happened. Bolan held his breath, hoping his lucky streak had a long run ahead of it.

His boat moved forward, coming about to slide in alongside the gangway. A rope was made fast. Up front the guards stood, shouting at the captives. Bolan pushed to his feet, moving in close to the captives, using the rifle to get them upright. He was going to have to play his role to the hilt until he got a chance to slip away once they were on board the ship. As the captives started up the swaying gangway, Bolan edged in among them, picking up the shouted commands of the other guards. He repeated what he heard, keeping his voice low and harsh. He watched the top of the ladder getting closer. There were members of the ship's crew at the head of the gangway, pushing the emerging captives along the deck in the direction of an open cargo hatch. Bolan kept up his momentum, and as he reached the top of the ladder he grabbed the manacle chain of one captive, hauling the man off the gangway, prodding him along the deck with the rifle. Turning quickly, Bolan merged with the shuffling mass of captives, working his way along the deck, pushing through so that as they approached the open hatch Bolan was on the inside of the line. He took a look at the layout of the deck. The area was as untidy as the outward appearance of the ship. It was littered with odds and ends of ropes and chains, fuel barrels and packing cases.

Glancing to his left Bolan saw an open bulkhead door that would lead into the main block of the superstructure.

The soldier moved to one side, walking in a direct line for the bulkhead door, and stepped through without pause. He found himself in a short walkway with a metal companionway leading to the upper level. He made his way toward it.

A figure appeared from the other end of the walkway. Clad in dark pants and a faded blue denim shirt, the man stared at Bolan. When he spoke, in a tongue Bolan didn't understand, the Executioner knew his cover was about to be blown. The man rapped out another challenge, and when Bolan failed to respond the man reached for the butt of a pistol he carried tucked in his wide leather belt.

Bolan took a step forward, swinging the rifle in a hard arc that connected with the other man's jaw, breaking bone and opening a gash that spurted blood. The man stumbled back, eyes glazing. He slammed into the bulkhead and hung there. Bolan hit him a second time, the butt of the rifle smacking into the side of the man's skull with stunning force. The slaver went down without a sound, his body shuddering. Bolan bent over him, taking possession of the handgun and pushing it behind his own belt.

He made for the companionway and mounted the steel steps two at a time. Bolan emerged into an area that overlooked the main deck. He could see the open cargo hatch and the captives being made to climb down nets hung over the sides of the hatch. The pair of boats used to bring the slaves to the ship was being winched back on board and the gangway was being secured. Bolan felt the metal decking vibrate underfoot. The ship's engines were being brought to life in preparation for leaving. He heard the rattle of the anchor chain being pulled up.

Moving around the side of the superstructure Bolan saw a companionway that led up to the bridge. He headed for it and climbed, using his boot to kick open the door.

There were three crewmen in the wheelhouse. One was at the wheel, a second man bent over a chart table, and the third, a bearded, black-haired man in a creased uniform, spun around as Bolan entered. He stared at the autorifle in Bolan's hand, his face registering surprise as the Executioner pushed back the hood of the robe and dragged off the turban headgear.

Bolan backed himself into a corner, pressing against the bulkhead. He gestured with the SA-80. "If you understand English this is going to be a lot easier."

"Who are you?" the uniformed man demanded in accented English.

"You the captain?"

The man nodded.

"I'm not the coast guard, but that isn't getting you off the hook."

"This is my ship. You cannot do this."

"I'd say I've already done it."

The soldier's eye caught the almost casual move of the man at the chart table. His left hand was easing toward something concealed from Bolan's view. When his hand rose it was clutching a stubby handgun and the man lifted it quickly, half-turning in Bolan's direction.

Bolan turned the rifle and fired, the 5.56 mm slug punching in through the hardman's skull. He fell with a lot of noise, leaving a glistening smear on the bulkhead behind him. The action broke the tableau. Bolan sensed the wheelman abandoning his post and lunging at him. The man ran directly into the reversed butt of the SA-80. It hit him full in the face, crushing his nose and tearing a bloody gash across his left cheek. The man fell back, howling, blood spurting through his fingers as he covered his face. Bolan couldn't afford to have too much interruption during his next action. He swung the rifle again, ramming it hard into the base of the man's skull, pitching him to the deck.

The captain's body slammed into Bolan. They fell against the bulkhead. The captain was not slender, and his heavy weight pinned Bolan so he was unable to use the rifle. Bolan resorted to cruder, more direct action. He jammed his knee up into the man's groin, hard. The captain groaned and fell back a step. Bolan repeated the maneuver. As the captain pulled away the Executioner raised a foot and slammed it against the man's stomach, shoving hard. The captain flew backward, slamming into the far bulkhead, his shoulders shattering the side window glass. He slumped to his knees, reaching up to press a hand to the bloody gash broken glass had opened in the side of his neck. The bright liquid squirted out between his fingers, pumped by his beating heart.

Bolan leaned the SA-80 against the bulkhead. He took the pistol he had tucked behind his belt and held it ready while he shrugged out of the robe, tossing it aside. Retrieving the carbine, Bolan crossed to the ship's wheel. He saw that the wheelman had already ordered the engines astern. Bolan used the engine-room telegraph to order half-speed. He felt the ship respond slowly and swung the wheel, bringing the vessel around. The ship moved with ponderous slowness, Bolan aware that every second counted now. Someone down below was going to see what was happening and wonder why. There was also the chance someone might have heard the shot or breaking glass.

Glancing through the wheelhouse glass, Bolan saw that the bow of the ship was pointing at the beach. He ordered half-ahead. There was a hesitation. Bolan made the request again. The ship's reverse motion slowed as it responded to the screws' change in rotation. Bolan felt the forward movement. He held the wheel steady, feeling the ship pushing through the water toward the beach.

The telephone began to ring inside the wheelhouse. A grim smile edged Bolan's lips. Someone had noticed what was happening, and questions were about to be asked.

He stepped away from the wheel, checking the SA-80. Any minute now he was going to receive visitors. Bolan un-zipped the knapsack on his back and pulled out a couple of grenades. He spotted movement on the walkway outside the wheelhouse. Angry faces stared at him through the window. Bolan figured the time for hesitation was long gone. He opened fire, pumping rounds at the windows. Glass shattered as the 5.56 mm bullets blew through. The angry faces turned bloody, bodies twisting as the slugs cleaved into them. Bolan's visitors went down on the walkway in sudden agony. The Executioner turned to the far side of the wheelhouse, using the door on that side to make his exit. As he stepped outside he heard the clatter of men coming up the companionway. Bolan moved to the head of the metal steps and raked the armed figures with autofire. Shattered bodies fell back, crashing to the deck below.

Hearing more noise on the opposite side of the wheelhouse, Bolan backtracked, peering around the edge of the window frame. Three armed men were staring through the far side. When they saw Bolan they pushed the door open and crowded into the wheelhouse. Bolan pulled the pin on one of his grenades and lobbed it. It clattered across the wheelhouse floor and detonated with a hollow blast. Bolan heard brief screams as the blast died away. Shards of glass and metal fragments blew through the front of the wheelhouse and showered the deck below. Men began to shout and scatter.

He turned and made his way along the walkway that joined the wheelhouse with the crew quarters farther along the deck. He was moving away from the cargo hold where the captives were being contained. As he crossed the narrow walkway, Bolan paused to drop his second grenade to the deck below, where it exploded among some deck cargo, spraying debris in all directions. He pulled a couple more from his backpack and repeated his drop, the deck starting to trail smoke into the air.

From below autofire was directed at Bolan, but his moving form was concealed by the metal walkway. As he ran he could hear bullets clanging against the underside. He reached the far end of the walkway and ducked inside a covered companionway. There were a number of cabins at this level. Bolan kicked open doors and checked the interiors. Of the six he checked, only one had occupants, a pair of the white-robed figures who had come on board from the beach. They faced the black-clad Executioner, reaching for the weapons they had put aside, only to be met by Bolan's own autorifle. He left the pair in bloody heaps on the cabin floor before moving on.

Though Bolan had been expecting it, the beaching of the ship took him by surprise. The sudden halting of the vessel as it became grounded shook the ship from stem to stern. Then it began to sway, tilting to starboard a few degrees in the shallower water. The stern swung a little as the ship settled. The impact, reverberating the length of the vessel, threw Bolan off his feet. He slid along the companionway, briefly helpless before coming to a stop against the bulkhead. He gathered his legs under him and pushed to his feet, feeling the slight cant of the floor underneath him. Reaching a door at the end of the companionway, Bolan kicked it open.

Autofire sent slugs clanging into the metal bulkhead.

Bolan dropped to one knee and returned fire. His second burst caught the shooter, spinning the slaver off his feet with his shoulder lacerated and bloody. The crew member dragged himself across the decking to where he had dropped his weapon. Bolan stitched him with a second burst, preventing him from getting his hands back on the rifle.

Stepping over the body, Bolan saw a metal stairway leading to the main deck. He went down quickly, pausing at the open hatchway to check the area. He was near the stern of the ship, realizing he must be close to the engine room. Bolan sprinted across the deck, feeling steel plates vibrating under his feet. Another hatchway swung open when he hauled on it. The hot, oily air rising from the depths told him he had been right. Peering down, Bolan saw a metal ladder that sank into the depths. The sound of the pumping diesel engines was loud now.

Bolan took three grenades from his backpack, pulled the pins and dropped the grenades into the depths. He backed off quickly, cutting across the deck before the grenades detonated. When they did, the initial explosions were followed by a deeper, heavier blast that shook the structure of the ship. A burst of flame and smoke issued from the hatchway where Bolan had dropped the grenades. He felt the deck ripple under him, some of the plates popping their rivets. Smoke began to curl from air ducts. Whatever Bolan had done seemed to have caused serious damage.

Now all he had to do was get the captives off the ship before anything else happened.

19

The beached slave ship became Mack Bolan's killing ground. His black-clad figure could be seen running through the thickening smoke, seen then gone. He used the deck superstructure as cover, working his way down toward the cargo hold that held the captives. His unexpected strike at the crew left them no time to organize. There was a grim purpose in the way Bolan strode the deck, his weapons taking on anyone who stood in his way. He used his supply of grenades to good effect, burning his opposition to tatters. By the time he reached the cover of the forward superstructure the opposition had been reduced to a stunned few who were scattering for the side of the ship and lowering the boats they had earlier been winching back up out of the water.

Bolan was in a less than forgiving mood. It was fuelled by shadows that refused to go away, specters hovering around him. Christopher Jomo. A true friend who had put his life on the line for a cause he believed in, who had died in a way no one should have to endure.

And a boy, a child named Chembi. Torn from his home, marched across a trackless landscape, chained like some animal and treated with less consideration. Pushed and beaten until his body simply curled up and refused to go on. His captors' response to that had been to leave him in the dirt to die alone. There had been no one to hold and comfort Chembi. Whatever terrors filled his child's mind, he had to endure them alone, knowing that he had died because he was no longer salable merchandise.

Once again Mack Bolan had been witness to the dark side of humanity, left to pick up the pieces and to grieve for the victims.

At least Jomo and Chembi had someone who could avenge their suffering. Someone who would make the heartless monsters pay.

Bolan stepped out from his cover, the rifle in his hands delivering the sentence to the guilty.

When the SA-80 clicked on empty the Executioner tossed the weapon aside and brought his Uzi into play as he crossed the deck and looked down on the slave traders. He had no need for the 9 mm pistol. Not for these men.

The sound of voices drew him back into reality and he crossed to the open cargo hold, staring down at a sea of dark, upturned faces. Men, women and children, packed together in the stifling heat of the hold. Bolan realized there were far more than forty people down there. The slavers had been on a run, picking up captives from various points.

"Anyone speak English?" he asked.

A number of voices confirmed they did.

"Get everyone out. Off the ship as quickly as possible."

Over the next half hour Bolan witnessed the emergence of almost a hundred people. Many of them had to be assisted, even carried out of the dank, stinking hold. Bolan moved among them, helping with the weak and the injured. The sight of these wretched people, scrambling for freedom, had a profound effect of Bolan. When he looked into their eyes, reading the misery and suffering they had endured, he saw the plight of so much of humanity. Slavery existed in many forms. And too much of the world's population was caught up in some form of it. Political, religious, moral reasons—all of those things taken to extremes that ensnared people against their will and bound them to a life where they had little choice but to remain in the shackles of their particular hell.

As long as he was able, Mack Bolan would do what he could to free those slaves. He didn't give a damn about color or creed. His only concern was to allow them the chance for their own freedom. At least to return to them the dignity that was the right of every man, woman and child. It was a thankless task but one Bolan did because he could.

The stronger of the captives lowered the boats and helped the others into them. They were taken to the beach and the boats returned for more.

Bolan prowled the deck, searching for Randolph Karima. He found the boy helping an injured man toward the side of the ship.

"Randolph."

The boy glanced up at the tall, black-clad American. Bolan had recognized him immediately. He was the image of his sister.

"As soon as we're finished here I'm going to get you home."

"Where's Katherine?"

"Safe with a friend."

"Will you help me?" Randolph asked.

Bolan took the injured man's arm and they moved him to the side of the ship. Picking a couple of men who could speak

English, Bolan organized a quick foray into the cabins. They picked up blankets and a number of first-aid boxes. The galley furnished them with food and water.

When they emerged on deck Bolan saw that the smoke at the stern was rising. Time was running out.

"Listen up," he called. "Anyone who can swim get in the water and head for the beach. It's time we abandoned ship."

One of the Africans said, "Some of us did not survive. There are bodies in the hold."

"I can't force you to leave them," Bolan said, "but right now we have to make the living our priority."

The African translated for his companions. There was a short discussion. "You are right. If we can come back we will."

Bolan and Randolph took the last boat out. Those who could not get in hung on to the sides for the short trip to the beach before dragging the boats out of the water.

"Look," Randolph said.

Bolan glanced back and saw flames rising from the engine-room section. Smoke curled out from weakened hull seams. The slave ship was rocked by an internal explosion that burst open the stern. Fire and smoke billowed into the air, rising, spreading.

As the sound died Bolan heard a ragged chorus of cheers from the assembled captives. They waved their arms. Some even managed a few moments of triumphal dancing.

"What happens now?" Randolph Karima asked.

Bolan smiled. "Good question. I'm working on it."

A group of the now ex-captives intercepted Bolan. "How can we repay you? If you hadn't come we would be on our way to the northern slave markets," one of the men said. "For all of us I thank you. We don't even know your name."

"Belasko. Mike Belasko."

The man turned and translated. The beach chorused to the shouts of Belasko. "You will be remembered for a long time, Mr. Belasko."

"Pity you won't be living for a long time, Mr. Belasko!"

Bolan turned and saw armed soldiers stepping into view from the cover of the treeline. The man who had spoken wore the stripes of a sergeant.

"All that hard work for nothing," the sergeant said. "Now put the gun on the ground."

20

"Colonel Chakra wants to kill you himself. No way. You killed my trackers. I claim first rights."

Bolan watched the squad moving out of the trees, weapons lifting. The sergeant who had challenged him carried an SA-80 rifle. He was concentrating on Bolan to the extent of ignoring the rest of the people on the beach.

"Your gun, Belasko. Put it down. I want your attention when I fucking kill you."

Bolan turned slightly, his back to the African he had been speaking to only moments before. There was a deliberation in his move.

The Uzi was still across his chest when Bolan felt the African's hand grip the butt of the confiscated pistol Bolan was carrying tucked into the back of his belt. Bolan listened for the click as the safety was released, then the African whispered, "Down!"

No waiting. No hesitation. Bolan took the moment as it was presented and fell to his knees.

The crack of the pistol was loud.

Out of the corner of his eye Bolan saw the uniformed sergeant arch back, a puckered hole appearing just above his left eye. Something dark flew out the back of his skull as he toppled over.

This was only a fragment in Bolan's mind as he swiveled his upper body and brought up the Uzi the moment his knees struck the sand. He stroked back the trigger and felt the SMG respond. On full-auto it spat out its 9 mm slugs, the weapon moving in controlled arcs in Bolan's experienced hands. He knew the Uzi intimately, was aware of its potential when used correctly. He took out the lead pair of armed men even while they were still in shock over the death of their sergeant. Death claimed them with just as much speed, bodies punched through and bleeding.

Bolan wasn't slow in seeing the other three starting to react. They began to break apart, one attempting to take cover behind one of the palms edging the beach. The Uzi tracked him, the first burst chewing splinters from the tree, then catching the man in the side and arm as he sought to conceal himself. He stumbled around the trunk, blood seeping through his uniform, weapon drooping. Bolan took him down with a final short burst to the chest.

Return autofire kicked up sand only inches from Bolan. The Executioner remained calm, bringing the Uzi around and capping off a burst that shredded the target's throat and shattered his jaw, knocking him onto his back where he lay, one booted foot kicking at the ground. Bright jets of blood fountained from the torn artery in his neck.

The single-shot cracks from the pistol brought Bolan's attention to his new ally. The African had adopted a shooter's stance, gripping the pistol two-handed as he fired on the surviving hardman. The rebel soldier brought his weapon on line and jerked the trigger, sending his burst over the African's head. Then a single pistol shot hit him over the heart, pitching him to the ground and it was over as swiftly as it had begun.

Bolan pushed to his feet. He turned to the African. "My turn to say thanks."

The man smiled sheepishly. He looked at the pistol, holding it as if he wanted it to disappear. "It is a long time since I used one of these," he said.

"Where was that?"

"I was in the army for three years. But I didn't like the way it was being run. So I left."

"What do I call you?"

"Jonah Okra."

"Glad you happened along, Jonah."

Okra looked at the dead men, then back at Bolan. "How does all this fit together?"

"There's a covert section in the military under Colonel Chakra working with the rebels. Trying to overthrow President Karima. The president's kids were kidnapped by the rebels. They wanted to force him to step down. But the rebels were hit by the slave traders and the kids were taken by them. I'm working for Karima. My job was to get his kids back. Only it got complicated when I found out Chakra was involved."

"So you have Chakra hunting you while you hunted the slavers?"

"Just about explains it," Bolan said.

Okra nodded in Randolph's direction. "That is Karima's son?"

"He's the one."

"How are you going to get him back to the city?"

"Jonah, you know how to come up with the difficult questions."

"Well, I guess they need asking."

Bolan had to agree. His next move would be reuniting Randolph with his sister and then getting the pair back to Tempala City to their father.

His thoughts were interrupted by a muted voice that appeared to be coming from where the dead sergeant lay. Bolan crossed to the body and crouched beside him. He realized the sound was issuing from a transceiver clipped to the man's belt. Bolan took the transceiver and turned up the volume.

"...in, Sergeant Masson. I need updating. Answer me, damn you!"

In the background Bolan could hear the familiar throb of a helicopter's rotors. Maybe he had found his way out after all.

Bolan clicked to transmit. "Masson isn't going to report. Nor are his men. You can come and bury them if you want."

"Who is that?" There was a hesitation, then, "Belasko? Is that Mike Belasko?"

Bolan smiled across at Jonah Okra.

"You have the advantage. Or do I make a stab in the dark and call you Chakra? Colonel, isn't it? If I don't have much respect in my voice it's because you don't warrant any."

"Is Masson dead?"

"How do you expect to take over Karima's position if these are the best men you can send? Chakra, if you want me, do it yourself. If you think you can."

Bolan cut the transmission.

"Was that wise?" Okra asked.

"Necessary. Chakra wants me and Karima's children. He won't be concerned about these people."

"Don't worry about us," Okra said. "We'll take care of ourselves."

He began to call out instructions and a number of the adult men made their way across to where the bodies lay and took the weapons and ammunition from them.

"For now we will stay here. Until we decide what to do. At least we can defend ourselves."

Bolan realized it was the best option. He had freed the captives. Now they needed to move on, to establish their freedom.

"If I can I'll send help when this is over," Bolan said.

Okra shook his head. "You've already done so much for us, Belasko. You aren't responsible for the rest of our lives."

Bolan brought Randolph from the fringes of the group. "We have to go," he said. "Time to find Katherine."

The boy turned to look back at the mass of people. "Will they be safe?" he asked.

Okra patted the boy's shoulder. "Worry about yourself, Randolph Karima. Go and find your sister."

Bolan turned, leading the boy into the trees, away from the beach. He wanted to get them clear away. The boy trotted along beside him, silent. After a few minutes he reached up to take hold of Bolan's left hand, gripping it tightly.

THEY HAD BEEN TRAVELING for just over half an hour when Bolan picked up the sound of the helicopter. It was coming from the northeast. The sound rose and fell, finally becoming a steady beat that grew louder. The soldier moved in the general direction the aircraft was flying. The forest had thinned out and Bolan made for a generous clearing where the open ground would expose him.

He pulled Randolph into the shadow of a wide tree trunk at the edge of the clearing. "Don't move from here until I call for you. Understand, Randolph?"

The boy nodded. He stared at Bolan, then asked, "Are these bad men?"

"Yes."

"You're not going away?"

"No I'm not going away."

The boy slid to the ground and pulled himself close to the tree.

Bolan edged away, breaking into the open. He caught a glimpse of the helicopter as it came into sight. It was moving back and forth in a grid pattern, checking each section of ground as it flew over. Bolan moved into the open, crossing the clearing at a steady pace. The helicopter passed overhead, still short of the clearing. Bolan watched it fly beyond his position. The turbine sound began to fade. He turned to cross the clearing again. He reached midway when the helicopter swept back over the tops of the trees and yawed violently as the pilot worked the controls.

The helicopter, a French Puma, dipped suddenly, angling in across the clearing. Bolan turned and ran, leading the aircraft. He heard the sudden hammer of a heavy machine gun. The thump of bullets hitting the ground was uncomfortably close. Bolan veered to the right, doubling back. Gouts of earth flew into the air around him. He took a dive that ended in a shoulder roll, bringing him into a sitting position. Bolan pulled the Uzi into firing position and tracked the Puma as it swept toward him, coming round so that the door gunner could locate his target.

Bolan had the gunner in his sights before the Puma settled, hovering no more than ten feet above. He touched the trigger and laid a burst into the door gunner's upper chest. The gunner grunted under the impact, falling back to hang by his safety harness, the machine gun swinging free on its rack.

The Puma rose, hanging twenty feet up.

Bolan, on his feet, moved around so he could stay underneath the machine, out of sight. The rotor wash pushed at him, flattening the stalks of grass in the clearing.

"WHERE IS HE?" Chakra yelled. "Where is that bastard?"

"Staying out of sight," Campos said. He had taken down an SA-80 from one of the weapon racks. He clicked in a magazine. "Simon, he's taken care of the door gunner. Now he's waiting for us to do something."

Chakra unclipped his seat harness and pushed his way to the main cabin. He freed the dead gunner from the safety harness and took control of the machine gun.

"Then let's not disappoint him," he snapped. "Get us down," he yelled to the pilot. "A few feet off the ground."

The Puma began to sink.

Chakra gripped one of the safety straps, leaning out to check the ground as the Puma began to descend. He had changed from the machine gun to the pistol in the holster on his hip. He swept the area with the muzzle as he searched for the man known as Belasko.

On the opposite side of the cabin Hector Campos was checking his patch of ground. He watched the rippling grass, flattened to the earth by the downdraft from the rotors. The Cuban saw nothing. He was about to say so to Chakra when the thought struck him. The American hadn't been seen running for cover, moving away from the Puma, so if he hadn't vacated the area...

"He's under the damn helicopter," he called out.

Chakra turned. "What?"

Campos pointed at the floor of the cabin. "Underneath. He's using the fucking helicopter as cover."

"Land," Chakra screamed at the pilot. "Now! Put her down fast!"

BOLAN SAW THE PUMA SETTLING, coming down on him faster than he might have expected. He turned and ran, clearing the underside of the fuselage in a dive that took him away from the helicopter's bulk. He turned over on his back, the Uzi already pushed out ahead of him, and caught sight of a lean, dark-haired figure in the open doorway.

It was Hector Campos. The Cuban saw Bolan's black-clad figure, flat on the ground, with a 9 mm Uzi tracking in on him.

Bolan saw a rush of alarm sweep through Campos as he stared at the Uzi's black muzzle. Bolan pulled the Uzi on-line, finger hitting the trigger, then watched the solid thumps hit the body as 9 mm slugs punched through his chest wall. The tearing sensation that followed must have denied Campos the chance to cry out. Bolan watched him stumbling back into the cabin, away from the open door as he fell.

The moment he fired on Campos and saw him fall back from the open doorway, Bolan rolled to his feet. He reached the Puma in three long strides, taking a leap into the opening. As his feet hit the cabin floor Bolan saw Simon Chakra swinging around on the far side of the cabin. The man had a safety strap looped around his left wrist and a hefty autopistol in his right. He wore combat gear, with the rank of colonel pinned to the lapels.

As Bolan caught his balance, Chakra leaned forward and swung a heavy boot in a vicious kick that caught Bolan on the right hip. The blow wrenched a gasp of pain from Bolan's lips. Chakra lashed out with the pistol. Bolan felt it thud against the side of his head, over his left eye. Blood began to run from the ugly gash.

Chakra swung his arm a second time. Bolan ducked under the swing and used the Uzi to deliver a blow of his own to the African's jaw. Chakra roared in pain. He slammed the butt of the pistol down between Bolan's shoulders as the Executioner closed in. Bolan closed his mind to the pain, using his bulk to push Chakra backward. It was only when Chakra stepped into empty air with one foot that he realized his position. He swung the pistol again, catching Bolan's upthrust arm. Bolan leaned back, pulling the Uzi around so the muzzle was jammed hard against Chakra's body. Bolan pulled the trigger and put half the magazine through the man's lower chest. Chakra was swung aside under the impact of the 9 mm slugs. He missed his footing completely and hung, suspended by his left wrist outside the Puma.

Bolan turned back inside the helicopter and moved up to cover the pilot and radio operator. They had become aware of the struggle taking place behind them, but it had all been over before either man could unstrap himself and reach the weapons rack. Now they were confronted by the sight of the tall, bloody American, his Uzi fixed on them and with a dangerous look in his eyes.

"Hands where I can see them at all times," Bolan said.

He backed away and pulled the sheathed knife he carried. Reaching up he severed the safety strap supporting Simon Chakra's lifeless body. Chakra fell to the ground and lay in a sodden sprawl. Bolan rolled the bodies of the dead gunner and Hector Campos out of the helicopter as well.

"Randolph, let's go," he called. "You can come out now."

Bolan saw Karima's son emerge from his hiding place. The boy ran across to the helicopter and scrambled in, trying to avoid looking at the bodies sprawled on the ground.

"Go and strap yourself into one of those seats," Bolan said.

Bolan closed the cabin doors, then eased himself into one of the seats fixed along the sides of the cabin, next to Randolph.

"What happens now?" the pilot asked.

Bolan took the map he had carried for so long out of his pocket. He showed it to the pilot.

"Get us into the area, then land."

The pilot glanced at the map, then across at the radio operator.

"Hey, never mind him, pal," Bolan snapped. "I'm the one who gives the orders now. You got any problems with that?"

The pilot shook his head.

"Then do it. Just a word. I understand compass points and I can read maps, so no diversions. This Uzi is loaded."

The pilot settled in his seat and powered the Puma's turbines. The helicopter rose into the air and swung around as the pilot set his new course.

Bolan leaned his back against the bulkhead. He ached from head to foot. The gash on his head was still bleeding and Chakra's gun butt had left him with a badly bruised back.

He pulled the transceiver from his pocket and placed it on the next seat. Once they reached the general area he would turn it on and see if he could locate the signal from the set he'd left with Katherine and Ashansii. Bolan glanced across at Randolph. The boy was asleep. Lucky kid, Bolan thought. Bolan could use some sleep, too. Later. His mission wasn't over yet.

21

Mack Bolan stood with Ashansii, Katherine Karima translating for him again.

"Are the slavers dead?"

"Yes."

Ashansii smiled. "Perhaps they will think before they come to Tempala again."

"They paid a high price this time."

Bolan was facing the Puma helicopter. The pilot and the radio operator were on their knees, hands behind their heads, just in front of the machine. A pair of Tempai stood over them, spears held ready if the men attempted anything.

Ashansii looked across to where the other children, grouped together, were sitting.

"We will care for them until they are returned home."

"It may take a while, Ashansii," Bolan said.

"Then we will care for them for a while. Don't worry, Belasko. They're with family now."

"I have to go," Bolan explained. "To take Karima's children back to him."

"I understand. Take care, Belasko."

Bolan moved toward the helicopter, Katherine and Randolph close behind him. He gestured with his Uzi and got the pilot and radio operator on their feet. They all boarded the Puma.

"Set your course for Tempala City," Bolan ordered.

The Puma's turbines powered up, rotors starting to spin.

"Can you get me to Government House?" Bolan asked the radio operator.

"Yes."

"Then do it."

The helicopter lifted and surged forward, gaining altitude quickly. Bolan kept an eye on the pilot until he was sure the man had the Puma on the correct course.

Behind Bolan Karima's children settled close together for the flight. They looked tired and worn, their clothing torn and filthy. Apart from the superficial aspects the pair seemed to have weathered their experience pretty well. There might be repercussions later as the full weight of the ordeal emerged. They had heard and seen grim things. Bolan hoped their youthful resilience would see them through the trauma.

The radio operator caught Bolan's attention. "I'm having difficulty getting through. The frequencies are all busy, or jammed."

"Let's hear," Bolan said.

The operator channeled the radio through to the speaker. He ran through the frequencies, letting Bolan listen in. There was a lot of interference, voices running into each other.

"This is the channel for the Government House communications center," the radio operator said.

Nothing came from the speaker.

Bolan's immediate thoughts were that something was happening in the city, and following on that thought came images of rebel activity. He hadn't forgotten the bomb explosion outside his hotel, the unexpected attack by the rebels, tied he was certain to the fact that Karima's kidnapped children had been lost to the rebels. Maybe they had decided to increase the pressure on Karima, especially since Bolan's intervention and his clashes with the rebel/military forces.

He sat back, telling the radio operator to close down.

"So where do we go?" the pilot asked. "Maybe those kids don't have a home to go back to."

Katherine made a soft sound in her throat as she heard the pilot's comment. She looked up at Bolan. "What does he mean? Has something bad happened at home?"

"Everything will work out, Katherine. I promise."

If there was rebel activity in the city, Bolan decided, then he had to stay away from Government House until he could make a full assessment of the situation. Bolan's problem was his lack of contacts within Tempala. He immediately deleted that thought from his mind.

He had contacts.

Ambassador Leland Cartwright and Phil McReady.

Cartwright's team had their base within the U.S. Embassy. If he could get the helicopter to land inside the grounds the kids would at least be safe there while he made his assessment.

He turned to the children. "It's going to be okay."

THE PUMA'S PILOT decided to play his stubborn card at first, refusing to take the American to the Embassy.

"What are you going to do, Belasko? Kill me and let us crash?"

"You could have the first part right, pal. Didn't I mention I can fly one of these things myself? So if it comes to push and shove, you're a disposable asset. I let you fly so far because it suited my purpose. Think about it while you're watching for the city to show up."

The pilot fell silent while he worked out whether the man was telling the truth. The American had proved to be adept at everything else he had done. There was the possibility he was bluffing. The only way the pilot was going to prove that would put his own life at risk, and he had no intention of doing that. He realized his only course was to do as the American said.

"We should be sighting the city in about ten minutes," the pilot said.

"Fine. Alter your course and bring us down inside the U.S. Embassy compound."

AS THE PUMA TOUCHED DOWN on the lawn fronting the Embassy, armed Marines converged on it. They surrounded the helicopter, weapons ready.

Bolan ordered the pilot and radio operator to the cabin and got them to open the side door.

"Step out, hands in sight," the Marine sergeant yelled.

"Do it," Bolan said and let the pilot and radio operator exit the Puma.

Bolan brought the children out with him. "Sergeant, these are Joseph Karima's children. Can you inform Ambassador Cartwright that Mike Belasko has them safe. He knows about me. So does Phil McReady."

The Marine stared at Bolan's disheveled appearance. Filthy clothing and hard dried blood on his face and head.

"Sir, I don't know who the hell you are, but it's for sure you haven't been on a picnic."

Bolan smiled. "Sergeant, you said it. Now what about Cartwright? I need to talk to him fast."

"Sir, don't we all. I guess you haven't heard. Ambassador Cartwright was snatched last night."

"Belasko?"

Bolan glanced up at the familiar voice. He saw Phil McReady crossing the lawn. The man smiled when he saw Katherine and Randolph.

"Jesus, you did it."

"What's this about Cartwright?"

McReady held up a hand. "Let's get these kids inside. Then we'll talk."

The Marines escorted the helicopter pilot and the radio operator toward the Embassy building where they would be put under guard. As the pilot passed Bolan he asked, "Was it true about you being able to fly the chopper?"

Bolan looked him directly in the eyes. "What do you think?"

INSIDE THE EMBASSY Bolan followed McReady to an office. Once they were alone McReady crossed to a steaming percolator and poured Bolan a mug of coffee. As they sat down facing each other across a large desk McReady smiled nervously.

"Leland's desk," he said. "Hell of a way to get to sit behind it."

"While we were flying in I spotted some smoke in areas of the city," Bolan said.

"Rebels hit around midday. Power station, radio and TV studios. All key points. Apart from that it's been a stalemate. Karima somehow managed to pull in a fair number of loyal troops, so the takeover has sort of come to a standoff."

"Do you know where Cartwright is?"

"Rebel leaders have taken over Government House. They have Karima, Raymond Nkoya and now Cartwright."

"Any threats?"

"They say they won't quit until Karima steps down and Cartwright accepts that all U.S. interests are withdrawn from Tempala. We step back from the copper deal and there's not going to be any U.S. military presence in the country."

"Public reaction?"

"It's sparse because the regular media outlets have been silenced, but the general feeling is the Tempalans, including a hell of a lot of the Kirandi, have had enough. They don't want any more unrest. The bombing did the rebels a lot of harm."

"But they still won't quit?"

McReady shook his head. "The hardcore rebels still believe that if they get Karima out, the country will back them. To be honest, Mike, I really think they've blown their chance."

Bolan drank his coffee. It seemed a lifetime since he'd had anything so good inside him.

"Any chance of something to eat, Phil?"

"Sure. I'll fix it."

"First a shower and a change of clothing. Then I need to talk to my people back home. We still have a communications link?"

"Yeah. We have our own power supply so the rebels can't touch it. Satellite link as well."

"Good."

"Before this all happened we heard about you identifying Chakra as being part of the rebel faction. How's he going to explain that away?"

"Posthumously," Bolan said.

BOLAN HAD A DIRECT LINE through to Stony Man. Seated in Leland Cartwright's leather chair, refreshed from a quick shower, a change of clothing and having his wounds treated by the Embassy doctor, Bolan completed his mission update for Hal Brognola.

"Now that Chakra and Hector Campos are dead, and Karima's kids are safe," the head Fed said, "you'd expect that to be an end to it."

"Not as long as Zimbala and Harruri have their hostages," Bolan said.

Barbara Price was also on the line. "We have confirmed reports of at least twenty dead. Civilians included, Striker," the mission controller stated.

"What's the sitrep as far as Government House is concerned?" Bolan asked.

"Small rebel force in control. Just sitting tight until Karima gives in," Price added.

"With Leland Cartwright in the middle," Brognola added. "How do we handle it?"

"You really want me to answer that?" Bolan asked.

"No," Brognola said. "And don't mention me by name."

Bolan chuckled. "Do I embarrass you, Hal?"

"I'm thinking," Brognola said.

"How are the kids?" Price asked.

"Tired, a little confused and scared. They don't understand why they still can't go home."

"They must miss their father."

"Yeah, well that's something I'm going to put right," Bolan said.

22

McReady had obtained floor plans for Government House. Bolan sat at Cartwright's desk, studying the drawings. It was helpful that Bolan had been inside the building. It allowed him a degree of familiarity with the layout. Even so he was going in without full knowledge of the killing ground. It wasn't the way Bolan would have chosen to work, but the situation called for a fast insertion. The longer the rebels had their hostages the more likely they might end up doing something out of sheer desperation if they realized matters were working against them. Bolan had no intention of letting that situation develop.

At the rear of the building were cultivated gardens where civic functions took place. The garden area was walled off, and trees and shrubbery had been planted to add to the ambience. The rebels were reported to have both building and gardens under their control. The Tempala military loyal to Karima had taken up positions at the front of the Government House and they had it under close scrutiny, with powerful spotlights trained on the building. Attempts to penetrate the rear of the building had been thwarted by a rebel sniper.

Bolan went over the layout again, his concentration broken by a tap at the door. "Come in," he said.

It was the Marine sergeant. He was a career man in his mid thirties. Bolan had learned his name was Glen McKay.

"I have your ordnance, sir," he announced.

"Bring it over," Bolan said.

He handed Bolan a folder that held a selection of photographs.

"President Karima and Vice-President Nkoya," McKay said. "I imagine you've met them?"

Bolan nodded.

"Okay, this is Leland Cartwright," McKay went on, holding up a photo of a tall, gray-haired man sporting a tan that would have had George Hamilton jealous. "And this pair are Zimbala and Harruri, our rebel leaders."

Bolan studied the images, etching them into his memory.

McKay was carrying a Marine-issue bag in his hands. He placed it on a side table, opening the zipper. "I had my guys strip and clean your weapons," he said.

He placed Bolan's Beretta and Desert Eagle on the table, along with their holsters. The Uzi came next.

"I kind of took a fancy to that 93-R," McKay said. "She as good as the manuals say?"

"Never let me down," Bolan said.

"And I'll bet you've put that to the test a few times, huh?"

Bolan inclined his head. McKay sensed the reluctance to take it any further so he passed.

"Half a dozen stun grenades," he said, placing them on the table. "You said no frags?"

Bolan nodded. "There could be friendlies in any given situation on this. I won't take the risk. Grenades have no conscience. They kill anyone who gets in their way."

McKay smiled. "Never quite heard it said that way before, but I guess you're right."

He placed Bolan's combat harness on the table and then a combat suit of Marine issue. "Yours was worse for wear, so we found you this. Hope you don't mind."

Bolan picked up the clothing. The combat gear bore a dark night/urban pattern that would be ideal for the situation they were going into.

"I'd be proud to wear it, McKay."

"You worked out your strategy?"

"This one is going to be strictly get up and go. No time for fancy planning and looking for the blind spots."

"The way I like 'em, Belasko."

Bolan glanced across at the Marine, confused.

"I'm coming in with you," McKay said. "Remember this is my bailiwick. If I let you go in on your own my days in the Corps are numbered."

"How about your superior and the ambassador?"

McKay inclined his head. "Let's just say they've developed a strain of what-I-don't-know-about-won't-hurt-me virus."

"Welcome aboard, McKay. Let's get this show on the road."

IT WAS COMING UP to late evening when Bolan and McKay parked up behind a darkened office building two blocks down from Government House. They had used one of the Embassy vehicles. A plain, unmarked Ford. McKay, who knew the city like the back of his hand, had brought them in by a circuitous route that had avoided the known problem areas of the city. He pulled the Ford into a darkened alley, cut the motor, and they sat in the shadows until they were sure no one had seen them.

"The main force of pro-Karima military are stationed at the

front of the building," McKay said. "My source told me they only have a three-man squad watching the rear in case the rebels try to sneak out. Sniper on the roof wounded two of their guys during the initial assault. Problem is they don't have that large a force after spreading the rest across the city to monitor the rebels at the power station and TV studio. They have others on all the main approach roads in case the rebels try to bring in reinforcements. I mean this country has a military force smaller than the National Guard in my home town."

"Consider that a bonus," Bolan said.

THEY CHECKED THEIR WEAPONS. McKay carried a holstered M-9 Beretta handgun and an M-4 carbine. It was a shorter-barreled, compact version of the M-16A2 developed for the U.S. Military. It was a handy weapon for close-quarter work. Bolan had his Desert Eagle and Beretta, plus an Uzi. Their hands and faces were layered with black camouflage paint, and both men wore black, knitted woolen caps.

"I'm with you," Bolan said as McKay led them down the alley, bringing them to a deserted parking lot at the rear of the office block. Because of the power blackout the security lights were off, leaving the parking lot in shadow. The only light was from the pale moon.

They paused at the far corner, checking out the way ahead. McKay pointed in the direction they had to go and led the way to the next building, hugging the base of the wall. Bolan kept a check on their back trail, his Uzi cocked and ready for use if needed.

McKay proved his knowledge of the city by leading Bolan around the silent buildings, easing into the bush that encroached on the back lots. If the vegetation wasn't cut back on a regular basis the forest would have swallowed the buildings and returned to its natural state in a relatively short time. The heavy growth proved to be a godsend to Bolan and McKay, concealing their stealthy approach to the rear of Government House.

Now they were getting closer they resorted to using hand signals. It prevented any talk being overheard. McKay pointed out the position of the three-man squad of Tempalan soldiers watching the garden area rear wall. Bolan acknowledged with a silent confirmation. The pair circled the Tempalan position and approached the walled garden along one of the side walls, out of sight of the Tempalan squad. They crouched in the heavy grass that grew in abundance along the base of the wall.

The wall was around nine feet high. Bolan slung his Uzi across his back, securing it to prevent it from swinging free and creating any sound. He signaled for McKay to give him a boost, and the Marine cupped his hands and raised the Executioner until Bolan could stand briefly on McKay's shoulder. Bolan reached up and caught hold of the top edge of the wall, using his own strength to haul himself up so he could peer across the wall.

The gardens were in near blackness. The moon had vanished behind cloud for a period. Bolan studied the cloud formation and figured they had no more than a couple of minutes before pale light showed again. He scanned the roof profile of Government House. It was a flat affair with a raised parapet around the edges. He took his time checking out the parapet until he spotted the armed man with a long rifle. Bolan checked out the rifleman. He was resting both arms over the top of the parapet, and Bolan caught the glow of a cigarette in the man's mouth as he drew on it.

Initial keenness at being given the task of watching for intruders had turned to semiboredom. The long hours were showing. It was close to midnight, and the lone gunman would have started to wind down, his awareness dulled by his extended stint on the roof. Now was the time to make their move.

Bolan pulled himself onto the top of the wall, keeping his eye on the distant sniper. The man showed no reaction, simply smoked his cigarette and was most probably wishing he hadn't drawn that assignment. Stretched out along the wall Bolan was rewarded by the sight of the figure pulling back from the parapet to raise his arms in a lazy stretch. The sniper stepped back, turning so that he was at an angle that had him looking away from Bolan's position.

Bolan took the rope from around his waist and lowered it for McKay. The Marine grabbed it and climbed the wall quickly. He lay flat as Bolan hauled the rope back up. Together they slid over the wall, hung by their hands, then dropped, barely making a sound as they landed in the cover of thick vegetation on the inside of the garden wall.

Using the deep shadow at the base of the wall combined with the bushes and trees, they closed in on the rear of the building. There was a concrete path that ran around the base of the walls. Evenly spaced large clay pots that held masses of bright flowering plants were placed along this path. With Government House looming over them, Bolan and McKay crouched in the shadows of the surrounding bushes and assessed their next move.

There was a substantial extension jutting out from the main building, situated midway along the rear wall. It had large windows and double doors that would be used to allow guests to step out into the gardens. The roof of this extension would provide handy access to the main roof of the building.

Soft footsteps warned the Americans they weren't alone.

They pulled back into the deeper shadows and watched an armed rebel moving in their general direction. The man carried an SA-80 rifle and walked with the measured tread of someone on sentry duty. He stopped short of the bushes, turning to make his return pass.

The Executioner made his move, reacting so quickly that McKay almost missed him easing from cover. Bolan's hand had already plucked out of a pocket the thin wire garrote he had brought with him. Stepping up behind the guard Bolan looped the wire over the man's head, snapping tight against his throat and pulling the rebel to his knees. The man struggled in blind panic as the thin wire sliced into his flesh. He was unable to get a grip on the wire as blood began to surge from the deeply sliced flesh. His legs kicked out and his arms flailed, but he made no sound except a soft, wet gurgling as Bolan increased the pressure. A savage twist rolled the man on his side, Bolan placing a knee in his back to hold him down as he applied the final pressure that ended the struggle. As the guard slumped loose and still on the ground Bolan freed the garrote and coiled it up, wiping his bloody hands down the legs of his fatigues. He caught hold of the guard's collar and dragged the body out of sight under the bushes, making sure he had the man's rifle.

Bolan signaled McKay to join him and they scanned the gardens, watching to see if there was another sentry. Time passed and then a dark figure came into view on the far side of the smooth lawn. The newcomer patrolled in the same fashion as his now-dead partner. Bolan allowed another couple of minutes to pass. No one else showed.

The guard made his slow way to the far end of the garden, moving across to the side where Bolan and McKay waited.

Eventually he was going to miss the other guard and sound an alert. Bolan uncoiled the garrote and slid deeper into the bushes, working his way down the base of the wall until he was behind the patrolling sentry.

McKay, who was watching the scene unfold, just caught a glimpse of the form that came out of the bushes. There was barely a sound until he heard the guard's choking gurgle as the thin wire in Bolan's hands flipped over the guard's head and sank into the soft flesh of his throat. The struggle was brief, ending when Bolan pulled the body into the bushes.

Bolan rejoined McKay. He secured his Uzi, bringing it forward before indicating the building. The pair made their way to the extension. Bolan pointed at the sturdy downpipe coming from the guttering. He boosted McKay up and watched the Marine shin up the pipe and roll out of sight on the flat roof. Bolan went after him and they hugged the shadows, checking out the distance they would have to climb to reach the main roof.

As they crouched there, listening, they heard the sound of the sniper moving back and forth on the other side of the parapet. McKay handed Bolan his M-4.

"I'll take this one," he said. "Cover me, Belasko."

McKAY LISTENED FOR THE footfalls of the sniper. The man was muttering something into a transceiver. He seemed to be having words with whoever was on the other end of the conversation. Maybe the rebels were becoming restless. Nothing seemed to be happening and they were getting into the late evening, a time when people started to get tired, even fractious. It meant they could be letting their guard down a little. On the negative side it also made them dangerous because a nervous hostage-taker was a risk. Tired, fretful people did un-expected things if they thought nothing was happening.

The sniper snapped something harsh into his transceiver, then moved to the parapet and banged the transceiver down. Still muttering to himself he fumbled in his pocket for his pack of cigarettes and drew one out. He tried to light it but the slight evening breeze blowing across the roof of the building snuffed the flame. The sniper turned his back to the breeze and hunched his shoulders, head down as he tried again.

It was McKay's turn to move. The Marine rose to his full height and caught hold of the top edge of the parapet. He shoved off the extension, heaving himself up until he gained a foothold along the bottom. Without pause he vaulted over the parapet, his soft-soled boots barely making a sound as he touched down on the other side. As he landed he slid his sheathed knife free and moved in on the sniper, who started to turn, sensing a presence behind him. McKay's right hand slid round the sniper's head, knocking the cigarette from his lips as he clamped his hand over the sniper's mouth. McKay pulled the rebel in close and brought the knife around in a short, hard arc, sliding it in under the sniper's ribs and into his heart. The rebel stiffened against the pain. He moaned, the sound muf-fled by McKay's hand. The sniper turned and wriggled, try-ing to stay alive, but he was already on the downward slope and McKay was able to lower the stilled body moments later.

The Marine withdrew his knife and slipped it back into its sheath, then leaned over the parapet and clicked his fingers. Bolan joined him, handing back the man's M-4.

"The plans showed an access door," Bolan said. He indicated the location and the pair loped across the flat roof. The door was slightly ajar, with stairs leading down into the building.

"I'm banking on them having the hostages in Karima's office," Bolan whispered. "That's where his direct phone line will be."

"They'll most probably have someone manning the communication setup," McKay said. "I've been in here before. I know where it is. You want me to handle that?"

"Volunteering, Sergeant?"

"Hell, yes," McKay said, grinning.

They descended the stairs and found another door at the bottom. Bolan eased the handle and the door opened without resistance. Bolan cracked it and peered through. He saw the passage he had walked along on his previous visit to Government House, with the doors to Karima's office at the far end. There was an armed rebel sitting on a chair beside the doors, his back partly toward Bolan.

"Com station is back the other way, near where the landing opens out for the main staircase," McKay said.

Bolan peered around the edge of the door. As McKay had said, the wide landing lay twenty feet away. From where they were positioned, Bolan couldn't see anyone guarding it. He eased the Beretta from its shoulder rig and set it for single shot.

"Subsonic cartridges and a suppressor," he explained to McKay. "I'll deal with this guy. You head for the com room. Once I go inside Karima's office it's going to get noisy. When hell breaks loose you make your play. And, Glen, stay lucky."

McKay grinned. "Surely you know the old Marine saying, 'You're not allowed to die unless it's ordered.'"

Bolan shook his head. "I never heard that one before."

"I know. I just made it up, but it should be on the books."

Bolan pushed the door wide enough to allow them through. He turned in the direction of the rebel.

McKay, his M-4 ready in his hands, went in the opposite direction. He flattened against the wall as he heard voices coming from somewhere on the landing.

Bolan had picked up the sound himself. He kept moving, closing the distance between himself and the rebel.

The voices on the landing became louder. Someone laughed.

The sound drew the rebel's attention and he casually leaned back on his chair, his head turning to see who was laughing.

He locked eyes with Bolan.

He froze for a moment, then reached for his rifle leaning against the wall beside him.

Bolan snapped the Beretta into position, gripping it two-handed, and shot the rebel between the eyes. The rebel's head snapped back, a glistening patch of blood and bone on the wall behind him.

McKay heard the subdued chug of the Beretta and didn't bother to look back. He had the door to the com room in sight. But he could also see shadows on the floor where the landing became the passage and knew that any luck he and Bolan might have was about to run out.

He plucked a stun grenade from his harness and clicked his fingers to alert Bolan. He showed the grenade to Bolan when the man glanced around. Bolan nodded, turning away, his hands already clamping over his ears.

McKay popped the pin and rolled the grenade in the direction of the landing. He turned his back on it, head down and covered his own ears. Seconds later the grenade went off, the sharp crack and blinding flash of light filling the area.

The incandescence hung around for what seemed an eternity.

Bolan and McKay, protected from the effects by covering

up, were only slightly dazed. It took them a few seconds to recover.

After that Government House erupted into bloody chaos.

23

Bolan had a flash-stun grenade in his hand as he booted open the door to Karima's office. He lobbed the grenade into the office, then pulled back against the outer wall, waiting for the blast. He saw the brilliant flash of light, heard the detonation through covered ears. As the sound faded and the glow receded, Bolan turned and ducked inside the room, scanning the interior to identify the occupants.

He was met by an armed rebel. The hardman was blinking, his watering eyes as he struggled to maintain his stance, the autorifle in his hands swinging about wildly. The weapon began to fire, bullets peppering the walls behind Bolan. The Executioner stayed low, his Uzi tracking the man. A short burst caught the rebel in the chest, knocking him off his feet. As he went down, his finger still jerking back against the trigger, a 5.56 mm bullet hit one of the office windows, shattering it and dropping glass to the square below.

Bolan was already moving.

He identified Leland Cartwright, bound to a chair, his face marked by a spread of ugly bruises. Behind him an armed rebel was frantically rubbing his eyes with his free hand.

Bolan took him out with a burst to the side of his head, spinning the rebel away from the ambassador.

Joseph Karima sat at his desk, both hands cupping his face as he reacted to the effect of the flash-stun grenade, and Raymond Nkoya was down on hands and knees, groping blindly around the floor.

Bolan turned his attention to Harruri and Zimbala. The rebel leaders were at the far end of the room, backs to the door in deep conversation, and had escaped the bright white burn of the grenade's light, although the concussion had deafened them. They both turned as Bolan came into the room, hands dropping to the pistols on their hips.

In the brief seconds it took for Bolan to deal with the rebel standing over Leland Cartwright, Zimbala and Harruri cleared their weapons and turned them on the Executioner.

Out of the corner of his eye Bolan saw the autopistols. He took evasive action, throwing himself to the floor and rolling frantically, hearing the heavy sound of the handguns. Bullets pounded the polished wood floor around him. Keen splinters smacked against Bolan's clothing. He felt a solid blow to his left upper arm and it started to go numb. The Executioner knew he'd been hit. He slammed up against the front of Karima's large desk and cast the Uzi aside, snatching the Desert Eagle from its holster. His left arm had lost all its feeling now and dragged along the floor as he moved to a better position.

Shempi Harruri rushed around the far end of the desk. His face was twisted in pain from his deafened ears. Bolan fired the moment he saw Harruri's feet and legs, placing two .44 Magnum rounds into the rebel's right thigh. Bone shattered, the power of the slugs ripping away muscle and flesh. Blood began to pulse from the pulpy, open wounds. Harruri fell, clutching the edge of the desk. As his upper body came into Bolan's target space he fired a third shot that punched through Harruri's forehead and shredded his brain in a shower of mushrooming gore blowing out the back of his skull.

GLEN MCKAY had seen Bolan vanish inside Karima's office. He picked up the pace and moved along the passage until he rounded the corner that opened onto the wide landing. The shadows he had seen turned into the stunned figures of the two rebels. They were trying to shake off the disorientation caused by the flash-stun grenade. McKay hit them with a burst from his M-4. One went down on his back, the other staggered across the landing before toppling out of sight back down the stairs he had just climbed.

By this time McKay had crossed to the com room door. He drove the door wide open with a hard boot, then stepped forward to face the room's occupants. There was the radio operator and an armed rebel and his rifle. McKay hit the rifleman with a burst that sent a line of slugs into the man's upper chest. They knocked him off the chair he was straddling, sending him into the corner of the room. The rebel tried for the rifle he'd let go of. McKay hit him with another burst that stopped him completely.

Turning the muzzle of the weapon on the radio man McKay caught the rebel picking up a hardgun he had beside him. The rebel swung the weapon around, firing a fraction too soon. The bullet passed between McKay's body and his left arm. Before the rebel could alter his aim McKay triggered the M-4 and put a pair of 5.56 mm slugs into the rebel's chest. The impact shoved him back in his chair and it rolled away from the desk, coming to rest against the far wall.

"Son of a bitch," the Marine muttered.

He heard the sound of gunfire from the direction of Karima's office, then picked up the clatter of boots on the staircase.

Company was on the way.

McKay stepped out of the com room and moved to the head of the staircase, meeting three rebels attracted by the shooting. He caught them midway up the stairs, raking the area with his M-4. The rebels were caught in the open with nowhere to go and not a second left to react. McKay's burst punched through their chests and threw them down the stairs in a bloody tangle, weapons bouncing down the stone steps behind them.

McKay positioned himself so he could see the base of the stairs and also keep an eye on the passage on the far side of the wide landing. With the bases covered he had time to wonder how his partner was faring in Karima's office.

HARRURI WAS SPRAWLED across the floor directly in front of Bolan, his body shuddering from the ravaging effects of the .44 Magnum rounds, his pistol slipping from his dead fingers.

Bolan had already moved around to the far end of the desk and then to the rear. He heard a scurry of movement as well as a sound of protest from Karima.

"Belasko, if that is your name, I have Karima. Do anything and I'll shoot him."

Leaning around the corner of the desk Bolan saw Karima's legs and the seat he was sitting in. Glancing up, Bolan saw Zimbala, one arm across Karima's chest, his other hand wielding a pistol. The rebel leader was in the act of bringing the weapon down to press against Karima's head.

Bolan had a couple of seconds to act. After that it would start to get tricky. His one shot at Zimbala had to be accurate.

The Desert Eagle rose in Bolan's steady right hand, tracked in on Zimbala and blasted a .44-caliber bullet that struck the rebel leader in the side of the head. Zimbala stumbled back, his shocked expression wiped away when Bolan fired again, this time laying the Magnum round in Zimbala's chest. The man turned under the impact, blood trailing from his shattered skull and chest, legs losing their coordination. He went down heavily, his pistol flying from slack fingers. It bounced as it hit the floor, spinning across the smooth surface.

Bolan pulled himself erect, leaning against the edge of the desk, his left arm starting to give him pain. He could feel blood streaming down it, dripping from his fingers.

"Sorry, Mr. President, I seem to be bleeding all over your floor," he said.

Karima was staring at him through watering eyes, and Bolan realized the man couldn't hear him. There was the sound of boots moving along the passage. Bolan raised the Desert Eagle.

"Belasko? You secure?"

It was Glen McKay.

"All clear," Bolan said, lowering the hand cannon.

McKay stepped into the room, taking a swift survey of the situation. "You're clear," he confirmed.

"Out there?" Bolan asked.

"No problems. Especially now the military just busted in through the front door," the Marine said with a grin. "I guess we shook 'em up with all the shooting."

They could hear shouting and the clatter of boots on the stairs, then approaching the office. From a distance they could hear the rattle of autofire. McKay crossed the office and used his knife to free Leland Cartwright.

"Hey, Belasko, you okay?" McKay asked, spotting Bolan's blood-soaked sleeve.

"I will be after I see that medic of yours back at the Embassy."

Armed figures filled the office doorway. A young officer stepped forward, scanning the room, his face a classic example of total surprise and bewilderment. "I think an explanation is in order here. Can someone tell me what the hell is going on?"

"Captain," McKay said, stepping forward. He offered a salute, which the officer returned. "You can let your people watching the rear know that the sniper has been taken down. We also dealt with a pair of armed rebels in the garden area. The communication room has been cleared, and President Karima, Vice-President Nkoya and Ambassador Cartwright have been removed from rebel hands, sir."

The captain, to his credit, maintained a professional manner. He turned to his men crowding in behind him. "Sergeant, room-to-room search. Flush out any other rebels. Secure the building. Have our communications team take over the com room and get signals to all our units. Inform them the president is safe and they can go ahead and retake rebel-held sites."

The captain turned back to survey the room. He took off his peaked cap and ran a hand through his close-cropped hair. For the first time he noticed Bolan, who was standing quietly to one side.

"Who are you?" he asked.

Joseph Karima spoke. Still smarting from the effects of the flash-stun grenade, he had recovered enough to intervene.

"Captain, he's with me." He glanced at Bolan. "Do you have more good news for me, Mr. Belasko?"

Bolan nodded. "They're both waiting for you at the Embassy. Probably sleeping by now."

"I owe you a debt I can never repay," Karima said.

"Seeing those kids back with you will be enough," Bolan answered.

"Time we got this boy back to the Embassy. In case nobody noticed, he caught a bullet," Leland Cartwright said.

"Captain, see to it," Karima said. "Mr. Belasko, we will talk later. It seems I have a country to get back on the tracks."

"If anyone can do it, Mr. President, you can."

Epilogue

U.S. Embassy.
Three days later.

"When are you coming home?" Brognola asked. The clarity of the connection via the Embassy communications placed him in the room where Bolan was sitting.

"Couple more days," Bolan told him. "Karima has things in hand pretty well now. Have to hand it to the guy. It's like he's undergone a transformation. Nearly losing everything, especially his kids, has given him an edge. And the country is behind him. Rebel opposition has crumbled heavily. The ones who haven't quit took off for the back country. Karima's going to have to deal with them sooner or later, but I think he'll come through."

"Losing Chakra seems to have taken the spirit out of the rebel movement," Brognola said. "Information we're getting says the military is in a state of shock finding out he was working against the government."

"Karima has taken over Chakra's role until he can find a replacement. He's coming down hard on the people who were siding with the rebels. Cleaning house has rooted out most of the rebel sympathizers."

"Cartwright is back on track with his negotiations, I hear."

"That guy is unstoppable. He was back at the conference table the next day."

"From what I heard from the Man, Cartwright is now a big fan of yours. Apparently you impressed him, and Leland Cartwright is not easily impressed."

Bolan didn't make any comment.

"By the way, the President sends his thanks. I also reminded him he owes us one for this."

"I hear one of the concessions Karima wants from the Navy is a couple of coast guard cutters so he can set up surveillance on these slave traders?" Bolan asked.

"Like you said, Striker, Karima is determined to make things work out there." Brognola paused. "Did his teams locate all the people you hauled off that ship?"

"They found them. They're working on getting them all back home."

"How's the arm doing?"

"Mending nicely. I was lucky, Hal. Luckier than some." Bolan was thinking about Christopher Jomo. And Chembi. The image of the boy, cold and alone in death, would become one of the ghosts that reached out of the darkness to remind Bolan why he continued his Everlasting War. Sometimes it had nothing to do with large-scale threats or the twisted plans of evil men. There were occasions when it had to do with the death of a single, innocent child.

And that was more than enough to keep him moving along that extra mile.

THE DESTROYER

POLITICAL PRESSURE

The juggernaut that is the Morals and Ethics Behavior Establishment—MAEBE—is on a roll. Will its ultra-secret enforcement arm, the White Hand, kill enough scumbags to make their guy the uber-boy of the Presidential race? MAEBE! Will Orville Flicker succeed in his murderous, manipulative campaign to win the Oval Office? MAEBE! Can Remo and Chiun stop the bad guys from getting whacked—at least until CURE officially pays them to do it? MAEBE!

Available April 2004 at your favorite retail outlet.

DEATH LANDS®

Hellbenders

*Available in March 2004
at your favorite retail outlet.*

Emerging from a gateway into a redoubt filled with preDark technology, Ryan and his band hope to unlock some of the secrets of post-nuclear America. But the fortified redoubt is under the control of a half-mad former sec man hell-bent on vengeance, who orders Ryan and the others to jump-start his private war against two local barons. Under the harsh and pitiless glare of the rad-blasted desert sun, the companions fight to see another day, whatever it brings....

Or order your copy now by sending your name, address, zip or postal code, along with a check or money order (please do not send cash) for $6.50 for each book ordered ($7.99 in Canada), plus 75¢ postage and handling ($1.00 in Canada), payable to Gold Eagle Books, to:

In the U.S.
Gold Eagle Books
3010 Walden Ave.
P.O. Box 9077
Buffalo, NY 14269-9077

In Canada
Gold Eagle Books
P.O. Box 636
Fort Erie, Ontario
L2A 5X3

Please specify book title with order.
Canadian residents add applicable federal and provincial taxes.

GDL65

James Axler
Outlanders

MAD GOD'S WRATH

The survivors of the oldest moon colony have been revived from cryostasis and brought to Cerberus Redoubt, leaving behind an enemy in deep, frozen sleep. But betrayal and treachery bring the rebel stronghold under seige by the resurrected demon king of a lost world. With a prize hostage in tow to lure Kane and his fellow warriors, he retreats to the uncharted planet of mystery and impossibility for a final act of madness.

Available February 2004 at your favorite retail outlet.

Stony Man is deployed against an armed
invasion on American soil...

DAY OF
DECISION

A Typhoon class nuclear sub has been commandeered by
terrorist dissidents. Halfway across the globe, members of
the same group have hijacked an airliner and rerouted it to
Somalia. Now the plane is heading toward its U.S. target—
with a nuclear payload. While Stony Man's elite cyber team
works feverishly to understand a blueprint for horror, Able
Team and Phoenix Force strike out from Afghanistan to
Siberia, tracking the nightmare to its source.

STONY
MAN®

*Available in
February 2004
at your favorite
retail outlet.*